⋆BECK⋆

BECK

MAL PEET

WITH MEG ROSOFF

CANDLEWICK PRESS

Copyright © 2016 by Mal Peet
Manuscript completed by Meg Rosoff

First U.S. edition 2017

Library of Congress Catalog Card Number pending
ISBN 978-0-7636-7842-5

17 18 19 20 21 22 BVG 10 9 8 7 6 5 4 3 2 1

Printed in Berryville, VA, U.S.A.

This book was typeset in Fairfield LH.

Candlewick Press
99 Dover Street
Somerville, Massachusetts 02144

visit us at www.candlewick.com

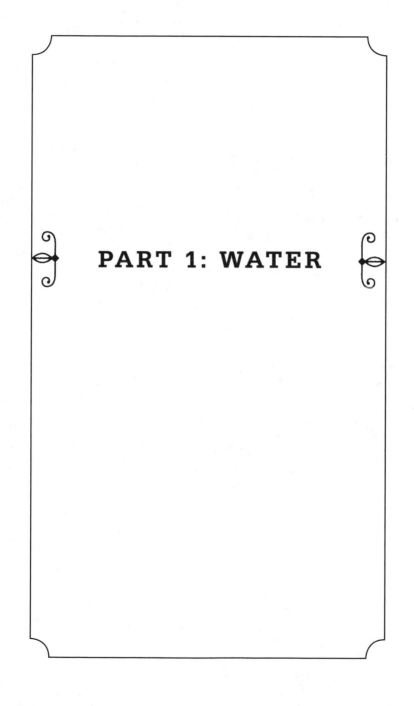

PART 1: WATER

1

AN ACCIDENTAL CHILD

HIS MOTHER MET his father in Liverpool on a frigid night in 1907. She was not a prostitute but in times of need, short of other forms of employment, she would sell herself to men. She never spent the proceeds frivolously. Every last farthing of the five shillings she charged would be spent on rent and on food for her family, which consisted of her frail parents, who were addicted to patent medicines, and an older brother who was wrong in the head. Thus she made financial expiation for her sin. Spiritual expiation took the form of full and frank confession through the grille of a curtained box in Saint Ignatius, a church distant from her neighborhood. She was a devout Catholic and performed her penances scrupulously. She would promise to sin no more, and meant it every time. Her name was Anne Beck.

His father happened to be standing outside a pub when Anne happened to be passing on her way home.

Twenty minutes earlier she had been sacked from her job as a chambermaid at the Imperial Hotel for slapping the undermanager who was groping her in the linen room. Beck's father was on the street because the pub operated a color bar, and he was African, from a country called in those days the Gold Coast. The landlord had refused to serve him. This often happened when his ship docked in England, and he accepted it more or less philosophically.

His white shipmates had protested but instead of moving on had brought him a pint and a baked potato to enjoy with his magazine serial in the drizzle. He'd perched the pint on the pub's window ledge, gripping the pulpy pages of his ha'penny dreadfuller in one hand while he gingerly conveyed the hot crumbly flesh of the potato to his mouth with the other. That's when Anne came by.

He was handsome and she was hungry.

"Wan' some?" Smiling at her, looking infinitely sad. Even sadder than she.

Anne shared his potato and his beer while he haltingly read her the adventures of Sexton Blake, and then she took him home. She was perfectly honest with him, telling him that it would cost money. He showed her the various coins he had in his pockets and she picked out British ones that added up to more or less five bob. She led him up the back alleys, lifting her skirt and alerting him to dog mess. They entered her house by the scullery door. Inside, it was quiet because her parents had passed out downstairs and her brother was locked in his room. She lit a bit of candle she found next to the sink and took him up to her room, where, despite her rudimentary precautions, he got her pregnant.

She never knew his name; his ship departed for Belfast the following day.

A month before Beck's eleventh birthday, his grandparents and his mother and his daft kindly uncle all died in the flu epidemic. Anne was the last to go.

Just before the fever stilled her heart she tightened her clasp on the boy's hand and whispered, "There's three pound and seven shillin' put away. It's in . . ."

He was an odd-looking kid with his mother's green-flecked hazel eyes and his father's coloring and hair that stuck out all ways. He was taken to the Catholic orphanage run by the methodically cruel Sisters of Mercy. His mixed race meant that he was also victimized by the other orphans. He lived in that dire and loveless establishment for three and a half years; at the end of that time he had become a hard little bastard who had learned to cry silently and dry eyed.

Christian names were not used in the orphanage and eventually Beck forgot that he had one.

2
THE LEAVING OF LIVERPOOL

O N A CHILL March morning in 1922, twelve of the boys, Beck among them, were led to the wash house where they had their hair cut off by Sister Francis Xavier, assisted by Mr. Joyce, the caretaker. Then they were made to strip naked and wash themselves at the long zinc trough, paying particular attention to their private parts. Still naked, and shivering, they were next intimately examined by a man who wore a white coat over his suit. The press of his stethoscope was like the kiss of a cold-water fish.

The boys assumed that these humiliations were a punishment for some as yet undisclosed sin, so they were surprised when they were then led to the laundry and issued with sets of clothes far less wretched than those they had discarded and boots that were almost new. Even more surprisingly, they were then taken, in their new finery, to the refectory and given a mug of beef tea and a hunk of bread apiece, which they eagerly and anxiously consumed with bald heads lowered. Eleven heads pale as suet puddings, one brown as a potato.

While they were chewing and slurping, Sister Thomas Aquinas came into the room with a clergyman they had never seen before. He had a face the color of canned meat separated from his black suit by a white collar that looked as hard and cold as the rim of a pisspot. He spoke to the boys at some length. Beck understood few of the words used. He had a vague idea what "adventure" and "opportunity" meant, but had no idea what "Canada" was.

At the end of his speech, the stranger ordered the boys to close their eyes and clasp their hands together. He recited a prayer. The boys said "Amen" into their empty cups.

The man regarded them for a long moment and said, "I envy you. Sincerely. Good luck, and may God be your guide."

At a gesture from Sister Thomas the boys stood. Very soon afterward — too soon for good-byes to friends, if they had any — the twelve Chosen Ones filed through the orphanage gates onto the street where, astonishingly, a green and black motor coach stood awaiting them. It trembled to the stumbling thump of its engine. The driver, a stout little man in a long brown coat, was loading kit bags into the boot. When he was done, he opened the coach's door, officiously, and the boys climbed in, followed by Sister Thomas. Beck had never before been in a vehicle of any kind. He sat near the front, gripping his seat against the noise and grinding rattle of the engine, and watched with fascination the way the driver worked the wheel, the levers, the pedals.

After a short journey that took the boys beyond the perimeter of familiar territory, the coach stopped at a building very similar to the one they had just left. It was the Christian Brotherhood Home for Boys, although no sign confessed the fact. Eight more boys with shaven heads boarded the coach, silently. One took the seat alongside Beck's. He smelled of fear and camphor mothballs and sat staring straight ahead with his hands knotted on his crotch. A priest followed the boys in and sat down next to Sister Thomas, who greeted him with a stiff little nod.

The coach set off again and after a mysterious passage of time joined the jerking melee of mechanical, animal, and human traffic that flowed and counterflowed alongside the river Mersey. The bald boys stared aghast from the coach's windows at a slow parade of massive buildings the color of congealed blood. In the gaps between them, stone-rimmed lakes crammed with ships, some masted, some funneled, webbed together with ropes. Rust-red cranes swiveled, their little cabins farting smoke. Man-high coils of chain. Carts and wheelbarrows and people. People everywhere.

Beck, uncomprehending, understood that this must always have been so, that this was normal, that this was what had been going on while he'd been slummed, bullied, confined. His heart, like his clothes and boots, felt too big for him. For most of the journey, he'd been gripping a metal thing next to a window of the coach. Now he realized that it was a latch that might allow the window to be opened. So he tried it and admitted a filthy spectrum of smells: dung, coal smoke, tar, brewery malt, tidal mud, fried fish, putrescent garbage.

"Boy! You, boy!"

Beck looked at the irate priest. "Yeah, Father?"

"Shut that fecking window, for the love of God!"

A huge building pale as early sunlight passed by and then there was the low expanse of the river itself, shimmering behind the dark filigree of cranes, glittering below a frown of cloud.

Soon after, they arrived at Huskisson Dock. The driver stilled the engine, used both hands to haul the brake up, and opened the door. At the priest's impatient urging, the children disembarked. While the driver unloaded the kit bags, the boys clustered between two enormous metal bollards and gawped up at the vast ship that loomed above them.

The priest stood aside and lit a cigarette. The ship's towering black flank was capped by a curving white superstructure full of small rectangular windows. Chains stretched landward from its nostrils. Halfway along the quay, a group of richly dressed women and men looked up at a car, a Rolls-Royce, being gently hoisted by a crane toward the upper deck.

It was not, of course, their ship. A uniformed man with a clipboard bustled along the dock and spoke to the priest.

Then he approached the boys and said, "Foller me, if you please, lads. Pick up your bags. Any one'll do."

He marched them along the pitted flagstones until they came to a hard-used vessel called the *Duke of Argyll* tethered to the dockside by thick hairy ropes. Jocular cursing stevedores were ushering complaining sheep into a wide door at its stern. A ribbed and roped gangway led up to a smaller aperture amidships. At the foot of it, Sister Thomas led the boys in a recitation of the Lord's Prayer. At the words "those who trespass against us," a hard rain began to fall.

"Amen."

Then the nun and the priest scuttled off, the nun raising her skirts clear of splash. Baffled and alarmed, some of the boys made as if to follow, but the clipboard man spread his arms to block their way.

"No, no, boys. Here. This way." He shepherded them onto the gangway. "Up we go. Single file, please. Hold the rope. That's it."

They all survived the slippery swaying ascent and were led along a metal colonnade, its white uprights lumpy with rust blisters, up a flight of narrow metal steps, across an oil-stained wooden deck, down two more flights of steps and through a steel door two inches thick. They found themselves in a penned-off and dimly lit section of the steerage deck. The panicky bleating of sheep was audible through the bulkhead. The space was minimally furnished with lockers and narrow high-sided iron bunks bolted to the floor. On and around these beds, another forty or so bald shivering boys were clustered.

For a moment, Beck was reassured; apart from the lowness of the ceiling, he might have been back in the orphanage dormitory. The clipboard man told them, more or less kindly, to make themselves comfortable, and that they would be fed and watered in due course.

Beck assumed they had been brought to live here in this unconventional heaving dormitory, perhaps because their previous accommodation was needed by a new flood of the parentless or unwanted. He was thrilled by the possibility of escaping into the nearby mad busy flux he had glimpsed from the motor coach's window. And by the absence of nuns. He was fairly sure that he could find his way back to the ramp and freedom. He chucked his kit bag onto the nearest cot, sat and waited for what he thought was the right amount of time, and went to the massive door. It was locked.

"Shit," he said, kicking the steel. *"Shit!"*

And when, two hours later, a mournful horn sounded and the room shuddered and an awful sense of motion transmitted itself through the unimaginable architecture of the ship, his cries of dismay blended with those of the other cold and hungry boys and the neighboring sheep. By the time the formidable door was opened from the outside and a voice summoned the children to supper, the tilting floor was slick with vomit.

3

THE LIFE OF THE WORLD TO COME

BECK FELT CONFUSED and astonished by the huge discrepancy between the solidity beneath his feet and the vast liquidity of everything else. The ship stood weirdly still upon a limitless range of green-gray hills of sea that slipped and bellied in all directions, leaving white skeins of foam in their valleys. Valleys slowly swelled into new hills to have their crests whipped by the wind into flying gobbets of spume. The sky was a gray parade ground across which stately formations of plumed clouds marched back toward Europe and home.

He stood in a loose crescent of boys alongside those members of the ship's crew who could be spared for the occasion. By peering over the shoulder of the boy in front of him, Beck could see that a sort of trough, a chute made of polished planks, had been angled down from the deck toward the restless water far below. It swayed slightly, upsetting his stomach. He looked away from it, to his right, and studied the man he now knew to be the captain of the *Duke of Argyll*, a man with a fancy jacket and cap, slightly soiled trousers, and a red beard like a rusty chisel. He had a small black book and a scrap of paper in his hand and was conferring with a younger officer, Mr. Mitchell, a man with a kind face.

The captain nodded impatiently and made corrections on the scrap of paper with a stub of pencil.

"So, it's *James* Riley and *Joseph* McAvoy. Not vice versa. Very well. Not that they'd give a damn now. Let's get on with it, shall we?"

Jimmy Riley and Joe McAvoy lay on the deck close to the chute. They were sewn into canvas sacks with their cold feet resting on lumps of pig iron.

The captain opened his book and began to read. "'Man that is born of a woman hath but a short time to live. . . .'"

That's for damn sure, Mitchell thought. Jimmy had been eight, little Joe seven. They'd died, stewed in their thin feces, quarantined in a spare cabin in the crew's quarters. Keech, the steward, had opened the door yesterday morning and recoiled from the stench. The boys had died holding hands. Mitchell's imagination refused to picture how and when that clasp had been formed, declined the question of which of them had died first and which of them had died alone. Quite properly fearing the spread of contagion, Captain Rennick had ordered the bedding to be burned in the ship's boiler along with the victims' belongings. The death cabin and the boys' quarters had been purged with Lysol. In a few moments, there would be no material evidence that these two boys had ever existed.

Mitchell tracked his gaze over the shorn children. They looked, as usual, numb and lost but none showed obvious signs of illness. Only Beck met his eyes, and Mitchell offered him a small encouraging smile.

"'O holy and most merciful Savior, thou most worthy Judge eternal, suffer us not, at our last hour, for any pains of death, to fall from thee.'"

Rennick paused, riffling through the pages of his prayer book. He glanced at his watch, then at the two seamen standing at the head of the chute. They stooped and lifted the limp bundle that was Jimmy or possibly Joe onto the boards and held it there.

Beck, at last, understood what was going to happen. He sucked back a swear word. His legs went unsteady, as if the deck had lurched.

"'Forasmuch as it hath pleased Almighty God of his great mercy to take unto himself the souls of our dear brothers, James Riley and Joseph McAvoy, here departed; we therefore commit their bodies to the deep . . .'"

Here Rennick nodded without taking his eyes from the page. The men at the chute released their grip. With a slight rasp and remarkable swiftness, the bagged and weighted boy slithered down and away and was gone. No splash was heard, perhaps because the sound was lost among the

14

susurration of gasps and faint cries from the congregation of children.

"'. . . to be turned into corruption, looking for the resurrection of the body, when the sea shall give up her dead, and the life of the world to come. . . .'"

The second corpse was now hoisted onto the chute. It offered some slight resistance; the mariners had to give it a little heave to speed its plunge into eternity.

Beck felt the press of something hard against his left arm. It was the head of the small boy beside him. He eased his arm free and tucked the boy's head into his armpit, cupping the wet chin in his hand like a football.

Rennick came to the end of his reading. He and his crew removed their caps and bowed their heads. The *Argyll*'s horn emitted a long, bovine moan. The stiff breeze keened and rattled through the halyards.

"Let us pray. 'Our Father, which art in heaven. . . .'"

The words choked in Beck's throat long before the tricky bit about trespasses. A voice in his head said, *Yer don' fookin' deserve this,* but he wasn't sure to whom it spoke.

4

CHOCOLAT

SEVEN DAYS LATER, after a slow progress down the fog-shrouded St. Lawrence, the ship's horn sounding its funereal bellow every few minutes, the *Duke of Argyll* docked in Montreal. Three-quarters of an hour after the ship's rumbling and nudging had ceased, Mr. Mitchell opened the door to the boys' quarters and stepped inside, smiling. The children were, as instructed, fully dressed, wearing hats and overcoats, sitting on their bunks with their kit bags beside them.

"Here we are, then, lads. Canada! A new life! And fresh air. You'll be glad of that, I dare say. Eh? So let's line up for disembarkation. Single file. Let's be having you. That's it."

Mitchell produced a purse from his pocket. Moving down the line, he gave each little immigrant a silver Canadian dime.

"Something for a rainy day, eh? Keep it somewhere safe. Not in a pocket with a hole in it, mind."

* * *

Beck examined his coin. On one side there was a bearded man; he assumed it was Captain Rennick. On the other side, some leaves. After a moment's thought, he bent and shoved it into his sock, where it nestled below his ankle-bone and against the leather of his boot. None of the boys thanked Mitchell, who was unsurprised; he knew they had little experience of generosity and scant practice at gratitude.

"Right then, lads. Here we go. Follow me and stay together. We'll get you sorted as soon as we're ashore."

From the top of the passenger gangway, Beck looked down at the group of adults who were clearly waiting to greet them. The women all wore hats like soft upended basins, long dark coats, and facial expressions suggesting that greeting orphans was not something they took much pleasure in. The two men wore gray suits, black hats, and clerical collars. Descending, Beck's stomach clenched. He farted, damply.

Mitchell shepherded the boys into a cluster on the jetty then shook hands with the reception committee. He took a sheet of paper from his pocket and unfolded it. Beck heard him speak the names of dead Jimmy and Joe. The grown-ups nodded solemnly. The younger of the two priests clasped his hands together and lowered his head. Mitchell took a pencil from his breast pocket and spoke again. The grown-ups gathered more closely around him.

This was Canada, then, Beck thought. It was not that different from Liverpool. It was as if the ship had gone full circle. A colorless sky. The same smells: smoke, tar, rot, salt, fish, oil. The same sounds: gulls croaking, beasts groaning, men shouting, water slupping, wind grieving its way through webs of rope.

He sat, *fook this,* on his kit bag. The coin in his sock felt warmer than his skin. He must have dozed, because the next thing was that he was looking up at the faces of the two priests and Mr. Mitchell's hand was on his head.

"And this sleepyhead is Beck. He's a grand lad, all things considered."

The clerics glanced at each other. The older one pulled the corners of his mouth down in a humorous grimace and rolled his eyes. The younger one said, "Welcome to Canada, Beck. I'm Brother Duncan and this is Brother John. We'll be looking after you the while."

Braemar, the Christian Brotherhood's receiving home on Rue Berri, was the biggest house Beck had ever seen. He had never seen a house with trees around it. Houses and trees, according to his understanding of things, had no business with each other. Where there was one, there wasn't the other. But Braemar had a huge tree—a great tower spreading dark green arms—between it and the street. And a row of wispy, witchy trees, misted with pale-green leaves, beside it. And bushes like huge green boulders in front of it. The house was (although Beck's imagination lacked the language for such a comparison) like an elephant trying to hide in, or feed on, shadows. It frightened him. He didn't want to climb the short flight of steps up to its doors of dark glass. But he did because no other option was available.

The doors opened onto a porch with stained-glass side windows that drenched the drab little newcomers in multicolored light. Brother John unlocked an inner door and ushered the boys into a dim, green-carpeted hall. Ahead of them, a wide staircase uncoiled its banister up into darkness. From high on the wall to the left, a carved Christ loomed down from his cross. To the right, a weeping but smiling Blessed Virgin gazed up at the top of the elaborate frame that contained her. Her tears were so realistic that Beck thought they would be wet to his touch, if he were tall enough to reach them.

To the right of the staircase, a passageway receded into an undefined distance. Some way along it, a door opened and another priest emerged. He leaned against the frame of the door and folded his arms. His hair, which was white, was at odds with his face, which was youthful. His eyes were a little too large for his face and were moist and slightly elongated. Combined with his lack of chin, they gave him the appearance of a kindly rabbit. And they focused on Beck.

He said, "Well, Brother Duncan, what have we here?"

"Allow me to introduce, Brother Robert, the new recipients of our grace. They are, in ascending order of height, though not necessarily age, Patrick Rice, Joseph Kennedy, Frederick Treacher, William Brownlow, and Beck."

"Beck? Has he no Christian name?"

"He was, apparently, baptized in the name of Ignatius, but he answers only to 'Beck.'"

Sullen, talked about, Beck thought he heard a child crying from another room. The priest called Brother Robert moved into the hall, closing the door behind him. The crying stopped.

"Well, boys, welcome to Braemar. We've never met, of course, but I already know two things about you. The first is that you are wondering where in the name of God you are. What kind of place this is. The second is that you have endured a long journey and are tired and hungry. Am I right?"

The ensuing silence was gravid. Beck broke its waters.

"Yeah. I'm bloody starvin'."

Brother John said, "Beck! In this house we don't—"

But Brother Robert, smiling, silenced his colleague by raising his hand. Still smiling, he went to a dark little table at the foot of the crucified Christ and picked up a small brass bell. He jangled it, and everything changed. Overhead, footsteps gathered like muffled thunder. A dozen boys descended and collided at the foot of the stairs. They paused briefly to consider the newcomers, then, cowed by the lifted eyebrows of Brother Robert, filed down the gloomy passage that suddenly ended in a blaze of light into which they jostled and disappeared.

"Time for tea," Brother Robert said. "Hang your coats up. Leave your bags. We'll settle you later."

* * *

The Braemar kitchen, Beck thought, was a sort of miracle. It was enormous. And warm. And smelled breadily wonderful. He found himself standing close to one end of a long table with chairs and plates and mugs ranged down its length. On the table, at intervals, there were loaves, platters of sliced cheese, and glass dishes of purple jam. The boys from upstairs stood silently along either side of the table. Looking up, Beck saw that a long wooden rack was suspended from the ceiling; from it, laundered shirts stretched their arms down toward the feast like hungering ghosts.

A stove was built into a sort of brick cavern at the far end of the room; on it, a fat black kettle pouted steam. A fourth priest — stout, with stubble-shadowed jowls — lifted it from the heat and emptied it into a half-gallon teapot.

"Right then, you newcomers," he said. "Find yourselves a place. No, no! Don't sit. Stand, like the others. As soon as Brother Robert comes we'll be saying a grace. Then you can get stuck in."

Beck slid a look at the boy beside him. Billy's throat was working like mad, swallowing saliva. So much food. And so close at hand.

The door opened and Brother Robert entered. His hand rested on the fair and fuzzy head of a pale child whose eyes were pinkish and swollen. The priest pushed him forward, gently.

"Go to your place, Alfred, my dear. There's a good boy."

Alfred went to the chair opposite Beck's. He kept his eyes lowered. He snuffled, once.

Brothers Robert, John, and Duncan took up position in front of the tall dresser that occupied the space between the two windows.

Brother Robert said, "If you would do the honors, Brother Michaelis?"

The jowly priest stood at the head of the table. He waited until the hungry boys put their hands together and lowered their heads. Then, at some length, he thanked God for the gifts hereupon this table.

"Amen," the boys raggedly chorused.

"Be seated."

Beck sat quick as a rat. He'd assessed the bread, counted the cheese slices, estimated the jam by spoonfuls per head. He'd lived on charity long enough to know the rules: eat fast, get most, remember the taste later. Don't be the first to grab, though. They like to punish you for that. The punishment for hunger is hunger. He watched the others. Little Pat Rice leaned toward the food as though he could live on the smell of it alone, but no one else moved. No one spoke. Vital moments passed.

Beck thought, *What the fook now?*

Brother Michaelis brought the huge teapot to the table and set it down. "Now, then," he said, tracking his smile around the table, "who'll be Mother? How about you, Victor? You've the good strong arms for the job."

Victor was an older and remarkably ugly boy. His hair

was bristles on a knackered broom. He lacked front teeth and his arms were too long for his sleeves. His wrists could have been knees on a normal person.

He said, "Aw, Farver. No' me agin. I done it—"

"*Victor!*" Brother Robert cracked the name like a whip. Then smiled.

Victor stood up and hefted the teapot. He carried it first over to the dresser, where he filled the priests' cups. His arms trembled with the effort of not sloshing the saucers. Then he went along the table, muttering abuse while he poured. Meanwhile, Brother Michaelis, using the longest knife Beck had ever seen, very swiftly cut the loaves into slices. To Beck's expert eye, the slices were of exactly the same thickness.

At last these tedious rituals were over. Seventeen pairs of hands lunged.

Brother Michaelis joined his colleagues. He sipped his tea then raised his comedic eyebrows.

"Well, now," he murmured with a small nod in Beck's direction, "*un petit chocolat,* eh? A first, I think?"

5
HYGIENIC BOYS

BECK AND JOE and Pat and Fred and Billy followed
Brother Robert up the soft-carpeted stairs.

"So, boys, are you well fed? Good. You'll have had a hard
journey. I know, because I've done it myself a few times
now. Back and forth to the old country. You'll be wanting to
get out of those clothes, too. Because, to be quite frank, you
smell like a pack of polecats."

At the landing he paused, backlit by ruddy light from
the tall window, and turned to look down at them.

"Over the years, hundreds of boys have passed through
this house. I cannot swear that all have departed pure in
spirit, but all have departed clean in body. Here at Braemar,
we do insist on producing a *hygienic* boy. Come."

The landing gave onto a corridor, closed doors on either
side — one, open, facing them at the far end, spilling light.

It was a large room unlike any that Beck had seen.
Its main features were warmth and an enormous roll-top

bathtub resting on four iron paws. At one end of this phenomenon a brass pillar grew from the floor culminating in a pair of fat taps that spewed water. Wisps of steam wreathed the oil lamp standing on the windowsill. The window was tall and blade-shaped, like in a church, and shuttered. Once-white towels hung from hooks. On the tiled floor, a rug with a squirming pattern of reds and browns and muted blues. Just inside the door and below the window, two armchairs upholstered like the rug. A smell in the room that was both sweet and as stale as snuffed candles. Brother John, now in shirtsleeves and a white apron, leaned over the bath, dabbling his fingers in the water. He turned off the taps and straightened when the boys came in.

"Right, young sirs. You've a treat in store. So, clothes off." He lifted the lid from a zinc tub. "Put everything in here."

Brother Robert sat in one of the armchairs and lit a cigarette. The boys stood, unmoving, uncertain.

"Sharpish, now," Brother John said. "The water's cooling. Don't be shy. You've nothing to show that we've not seen before. Isn't that so, Brother Robert?"

From behind his veil of mist and smoke the kindly rabbit said, "I should be most surprised if they had."

The boys undressed. Little Pat fumbled it, and, sighing theatrically, Brother John stooped to help him with the buttons. Naked, Beck and Billy covered their genitals with their hands. Pat put his thumb in his mouth. A silent stillness in the steamy room while the priests perused the children.

25

Then Brother John said, quietly, "Good. Into the bath then."

Beck said, "Aller us together?"

Brother Robert chuckled. "Oh, there's plenty of room. This is the leviathan of baths. We've known it swallow ten boys at a go, never mind five. Have we not, Brother John?"

"Indeed we have. At a squeeze."

The bath was so high-sided that Pat needed a helping hand to get in. None of the boys had previously experienced immersion in warm water. Billy sat at the curved end of the bath with his gob open and his eyes shut like a dreamer, clutching the sides. Fred and Joe stayed on their knees, trying not to get wet. Beck sat below the taps, enrapt, watching his submerged body become strange, feeling the heat soak into him. Pat howled when the water rose to his thin neck, and struggled upright. Beck yanked him back down.

"Is aw right, Pat. Hush. Yer'll never drown in here."

Brother John beamed down at them, his face flushed pink above the swell of his apron, an ingot of yellow soap in his hand.

"Isn't that nice? You just enjoy it. A little taste of heaven, is a hot bath. Now, I'm going to lather your heads. Keep your eyes shut while I'm about it, or they'll sting like the devil. I'll start with you, *Chocolat*."

Beck felt a drench of hot water and the hard rub of the soap on his scalp, then the priest's fingers working over his head like a blind man's investigation. He resisted the deliciousness of it, clamped his eyes tight against the sudden burning memory of his mother. Then a great slosh of water and he was awake again, eyes burning, gasping.

Brother John moved on to Pat, who sobbed and spat throughout the whole business. Billy sat upright with his face tucked tight as a cat's arse while Brother John did him. Beck thought that was the end of it, but it wasn't.

Brother John dropped a threadbare face flannel onto each boy. "Now wash. Tip to toe and everywhere in between. Face and in the ears. Don't forget your downstairs bits, fore and aft. Then legs and feet and between the toes. Off you go."

He went to a tall black cupboard and withdrew from it a bottle of whiskey and two glasses. He poured Brother Robert a measure and then another for himself, which he took to the other chair and settled himself. Brother Robert lit another cigarette without taking his eyes from the boys in the bath.

Beck had no words for what he felt. *Delight* might have been one of them, but he'd never had occasion to need it or know it. *Trepidation,* another. Sister Francesca, that ugly bitch, had many times told him that he was going to get into hot water. But he never had been until now. He squeezed the flannel on his shoulders and felt the lovely trickles of heat go down his back. He worked the flannel over himself. He pushed his toes into Pat's slatty little ribs and laughed when Pat flinched and sputtered.

"Enjoying yourself, *Chocolat*? Beck?"

He looked through the steam at the smiling priest. "Yeah. I'm well enough, ta."

"Excellent. Now, I want you all to sit and soak while you listen to what I'm going to tell you. You may not understand everything I say, but I want you to remember it because you will understand when you are older." Brother Robert paused to sip whiskey and draw on his cigarette.

"You are now at the point at which your old lives end and your new lives begin. This bath is the baptism that marks that change. It washes away the shame and hardship that has been the story of your lives so far. You will leave this house cleansed, ready to start afresh. From here, you will be sent to new homes. You will become members of families. Families who will care for you, adopt you as their sons. Most will be farmers who need your help. Yes, your *help*. I know that you are city boys who wouldn't know one end of a plow from the other. But you will learn. You will learn skills; you will become men who will shape the destiny of this young and magnificent country."

Brother Robert rested his cigarette in the cut-glass ashtray on the arm of his chair while he wiped a bead of sweat from his forehead. "I cannot say exactly when you will leave us to embark on these great adventures. You may be with us for weeks or months. But here is the important thing. While you are with us, you must forget the past. You will not be returning to that misery. And you must not worry about the future, even though it might frighten you. You have had the great good fortune to find yourselves, for now, in a place of safety. I and my fellow Brothers are inspired by the words of Our Lord Jesus Christ, who said, 'Suffer the little children to come unto me.' Our duty is to love boys such as yourselves. My years of service have taught me that you are unlikely to know what love is and ignorant of the forms it might take. So let us teach you, just as we feed and care for you. And when you leave here, take the experience of love with you. Keep it in a secret place in your hearts, just as you have kept Mr. Mitchell's dimes concealed in your clothes."

Fook, Beck thought, and turned to look at the metal bin.

Brother John laughed. "Don't worry, *Chocolat.* We're not going to take your hidden treasure from you. It'll be in your pocket when you leave. Now then, all good things come to an end, so out you get. There are other boys waiting on their bath."

He handed them each a towel then went to the black cupboard from which he took five folded white nightshirts. Dry, more or less, the boys put them on. Pat's reached to the floor. Billy's, Fred's, and Joe's came to their ankles. Beck's stopped just below his knees.

"You have become angels," Brother Robert said, studying them. "Now, down to the kitchen with you for hot milk. Then bed. One of us will come to your rooms to supervise your prayers."

At the doorway, Beck turned. Brother Robert had removed his jacket and was unfastening his clerical collar. "Go," he said.

*　*　*

Later, Beck and Billy were taken to a bedroom on the second floor. There were four beds; the other two were occupied by ugly Victor and a younger boy.

When prayers were over and Brother Duncan had left, when his footfalls had retreated downstairs, Beck said, "Aw right here, lads, then, is it? Yer get a feed like that every day an' that? We landed on our feet, or what?"

Silence. The skylight threw a pale-blue rhomboid onto the younger boy's bed.

"Lads?"

Without lifting his head, Victor said, "I'm outta here tomorrer."

"Yeah? Where' yer goin'?"

"Don' know, don' care. Fuck'm."

"Wha's that serposed to mean?"

Beck was startled when Victor sat suddenly upright.

"Wos yer name? Beck, ennit? Right. Aw right. Lissen. All yer need to know is this. Do wharever they want yer to do. 'Cause if yer don', they take yer down to the cellar. An' yer don' wanna go down there. Tha's right, ennit, Stevie?"

The boy in the moon-splashed bed silently pulled his blanket over his face.

"Yeah," Victor said and dumped his improbable head back onto his pillow.

"No one's takin' me nowheres I don' wanna go," Beck said.

Victor's laugh was short and without mirth.

6
PARADISE

OVER THE FOLLOWING days a kind of bafflement took hold of Beck. The mornings were not unlike those back in the orphanage. After a breakfast of porridge and tea, chores: washing up, sweeping, peeling potatoes for the midday meal; scrubbing the lavatories behind the scullery; pounding soiled sheets and clothes in tubs of scummy water with a heavy wooden paddle. The afternoons, though, were a departure from what he'd previously known.

After lunch on days of good weather, the boys would be divided into two cohorts and would go outdoors. One clutch of boys would be taken by Brother Duncan to the grounds fronting the house. Using unfamiliar implements, they would cut grass, trim shrubbery, rake gravel. When these tasks were completed, there would be games. Brother Duncan would initiate giggly sessions of hide-and-seek, or ball games with puzzling rules. At such times, passersby— ladies, mostly—would pause beyond the railings to watch and smile. Beck was often the focus of their pleasant attention.

Meanwhile, Brother Michaelis would take the other boys into the garden at the rear of Braemar: half an acre of ground devoted to the cultivation of fruit and vegetables. The two groups of children were alternated between these different activities, and Beck was hard put to decide which he preferred. He was dominant in the games on the lawn and, although separated from it by high iron railings, delighted in being close to the world of the street—the horse-drawn cabs with ribbed canvas roofs, the motor vehicles, the admiration of strangers with real and unimaginable lives. But the garden was magical. It was enclosed by stone walls too high to see over. The shorter wall at the far end had a low door at its center, heavily padlocked. One of the long walls was webbed with carefully crucified fruit trees nubbled with tiny buds. The other supported the lean-to greenhouse in which Brother Michaelis lovingly nurtured seedlings.

He led the boys along the benches, picking up seed trays. "Carrots, my scallywags. Like teeny green feathers, are they not? Loves a light soil, your carrot. Later we'll dig more sand into their bed. Now, these are beets. Beautiful purple veins they'll have in their leaves when they're bigger. And these little fellows are beans."

Beck liked the moist warmth in the greenhouse and, although to his eye one tray of seedlings looked the same as the next, he was intrigued by the notion that they would turn into things you could eat. Until now, the provenance of food had never greatly interested him; what mattered was getting enough of it. When Brother Michaelis's back was turned, he plucked out a plantlet, nipped off its mucky root, and ate the leaves. A flicker of bitterness on his tongue, then nothing.

Ineptly—not one of them had previously held a spade or fork or hoe—the boys worked the plots. Making faces, pretending to gag, they spread rotted horse dung and compost onto newly tilled soil.

On his fifth afternoon in the garden, Beck paused in his work. Spring had arrived, provoking birds into exchanging reckless invitations and challenges. The warmth spilling into the garden ripened the scents of greenery and turned earth. Like several of the other boys, Beck had stripped to his shirt and rolled up his sleeves. Ticklish sweat was gathering on his scalp beneath his regrowing tufts. He watched, smiling, a half-wit boy called Malcolm gently interrogating the large worm that writhed on the palm of his hand.

He moved his eyes over the even rows of pale-green shoots, each one forcing its way out of the darkness toward the sun. And cautiously, suspicious of what was swelling around his heart, he acknowledged that he might be happy. It felt like a special kind of tiredness, a waking sleep. He closed his eyes. Then felt the soft weight of a hand on his shoulder.

"Paradise, eh, *Chocolat*? You'll know the word?"

"Yeah, Father. It's where we go when we die, so they say."

"So it is, indeed. Good boy. But the word *paradise* means, literally, 'a walled garden.' Did you know that? No, of course not. But what we have tried to create here is a humble version of the paradise that surely awaits us. A practice run for heaven, in a manner of speaking." Brother Michaelis turned Beck around to face him. "And, as in the paradise that awaits us, there is no sin here. Unless, of course, you're bringing it with you." The Brother smiled and tapped Beck's stubbled head with a forefinger. "In here. Do you have sin on your mind, *Chocolat*? Do your thoughts dwell upon wickedness at all?"

"I don' think so, Father."

"Good. Because surely a sinful mind will find sin where none exists. Or as the great Shakespeare observes, 'There is nothing either good or bad, but thinking makes it so.' Hmm? Now, shall we get this bed weeded before the Lord gathers us home? Or before teatime at the very least?"

So the days were strange but good. Yet at the waning of each one, when Braemar gathered its shadows in, the mood within the house changed like subtle weather. The other boys, who had whooped and laughed on the lawn or chaffed each other in the garden, fell silent as they soaped their hands in the scullery. During the prolonged ritual that preceded tea, they sat with their eyes lowered as if the food in front of them were a kind of penitence. Later, after the chores of clearing away and washing up, a boy or two would be summoned to the bathroom. A boy or two would be taken to Brother Robert's study where, sometimes, they would have their futures revealed to them and leave Braemar the following day. Inevitably they returned late, red-eyed and silent.

The others gathered in the big front room and sat on the floor, shiftily cross-legged, for bedtime stories. These varied according to which of the Brothers was reading. Brother Duncan favored seagoing adventures in which male companions triumphed over dastardly villainy. He was good at voices: Scottish one minute, French the next. Brother John read tales of ancient wars or weird stories in which mad gods turned into eagles and carried boys skyward in their claws.

Beck was averse to books. They were full of wasps called *words* that swarmed at your head for no good reason. Gradually, however, and despite the fact that there were as many words he did not know as words he did, he became entranced by these stories. He would gaze up, agape, at the reader, and when Brother Duncan took a class of the young ones to teach letters, Beck lingered at the doorway so uncomfortably and for so long that at last he was invited in to join the lesson. Thus did he learn to read—not well, for the education of boys destined for lives of work and hardship was not a priority—but enough so that week by week, familiar words began to appear in his Sunday hymnal, and then sentences, until, to his shock and delight, he could find the meanings hidden on the page.

In the nights, there were cries and weeping. These did not trouble Beck unduly; they had been the nocturnal music in his Liverpool orphanage and on his voyage across the Atlantic. He knew that everything in life came at a price, and that there was bound to be one here.

Boys went away, new boys arrived, but Beck stayed on. One evening he realized that little Pat Rice had disappeared.

"He's gone to the Rancurlie Receiving Home," Brother Duncan said. "Where his brother is. We couldn't stand his sniveling a moment longer."

Three nights later, Billy Brownlow and another boy were taken to Brother Robert's study in their nightshirts.

When Billy came up to the bedroom, Beck said, "What's on, Billy?"

"I'm away tomorrer."

"What d'yer mean, away? Away where?"

"Dunno. Some farm somewhere."

"Some farm somewhere? They must've fookin' tole yer where it is."

"Carn remember. Onterrier, somethin' like that." Billy sat on his bed, looking ghostly and sick.

"It'll be aw right, Billy."

"Yeah."

Brother Duncan came into the room and clapped his hands together softly. "Time for prayers, boys. On your knees, now. Good. That's lovely."

When the lights were out, Billy whispered, "Beck?"

"Yeah?"

"He had me sittin' on his lap. Like he was me da."

"I never knew yer had a da, Billy."

"I didn'."

The following morning, Beck came from the scullery into the hall and saw Billy standing by the front door bundled up in a coat and wearing a cap. A cardboard label hung from the buttonhole of his collar. A kit bag sat slumped at his feet.

"Yer all set, then?"

Billy nodded, looking at the floor.

"Yer'll be fine, Billy. Yer will now." Beck put his hand on the younger boy's shoulder. It was all he could think of to do as a gesture of encouragement.

Billy sniffed. He wiped his nose on his sleeve then looked up at Beck and held his hand out. Surprised, Beck took it and the boys shook hands like men.

Brother John, humming jauntily but tunelessly, appeared and, with his hand on the nape of the boy's neck, ushered Billy out into the day's raw sunlight. Beck never saw him again.

7
BAPTISM

BECK WAS IN his nightshirt when Brother Michaelis appeared in the bedroom doorway.

"Bath, *Chocolat*."

The regular ritual was the source of mixed feelings for Beck. He loved the sensual feel of the hot water; he loved the fact that once or twice a month even his bones felt warm. What he didn't love was the audience of Brothers drinking whiskey and murmuring to each other as the boys bathed. Beck didn't know why it worried him exactly, but he had something of an idea. He wasn't a fool.

In the darkening passageway leading to the bathroom, Brother Michaelis came to a halt and clasped Beck's shoulder. "You're a good boy, *Chocolat*. We had our doubts when you arrived. But you have behaved yourself. You work hard. We are pleased with you. Brother Robert is *very* pleased with you."

Beck, unfamiliar with the flavor of praise, could think

of nothing to say. Brother Michaelis opened the last door. Beck entered. It closed and clicked behind him. The lamplight was dimmer than last time, the steam scented with something sickly sweet.

For the first time ever, Brother Robert was in the bath. Without spectacles, his big pink eyes made him look even more like a rabbit. His hair was wet and sleek. He was washing his neck and shoulders with a sponge. Foam dribbled down the Brother's narrow chest. Between spread legs his penis drifted above the dark mat of his pubic hair like the thick rufous tendril of an aquatic plant.

Beck jerked his gaze away from it. In his head, a voice not unlike his own blurted, *Jaysus, yer lookin' at a priest in the nip!* He turned to look for help from Brother Michaelis, who was not there. He tried to open the door but it was locked.

"What's the matter?" Brother Robert asked mildly.

Beck kept his face to the door. "I'm sorry, Father. I didn' know yer was in here."

"Well, I am. So take that nightshirt off and get yourself in. There's plenty of room."

"I'm fine as I am, thanks, Father. I'm not too bad."

"I'm not asking you, *Chocolat*. I'm telling you." The chill in the voice cut through the room's heat.

Beck was paralyzed. No, not paralyzed. His mind raced and there was a shake running up his legs all the way to his bladder. He knew the reckoning had come and prayed that the form it took would be somehow tolerable.

He peeled the reeking socks from his feet, hoisted the nightshirt over his head, and got into the bath, steadying himself with one hand on its rim and the other shielding his private parts. The priest drew his knees up to make room but Beck sat as far away as possible, below the taps, with his hands clasping his knees together and his eyes going everywhere except in the direction of Brother Robert's crotch. The sponge hung in the water between them like a drowned brain.

"Dear God," the Brother said softly. "You're not afraid of me, surely?"

"I ain't," Beck lied.

"Good. You have no reason to be."

Brother Robert took a bar of soap from a dish and inhaled its aroma. "This is not the terrible old carbolic Brother John scoured you with. This is the good stuff. French. *Savon de muguet,* they call it. Lily of the valley. Here, have a sniff."

Beck gripped hold of the side and leaned forward without moving from his position by the taps. "It's nice, Father."

"I like to think of it as the scent of innocence, *Chocolat.* Which is appropriate, for here we are, like two Adams before the Fall." He relathered the sponge. "Come forward so I can reach you. More. That's it. Close your eyes. Even the lily of the valley has a sting."

Beck felt the priest's left hand take the back of his neck and then the soft rough texture of the sponge slither over his head and face. Anxiety mixed with warmth and the intoxicating smell of the soap. He panicked, pulled away, spluttering, cupping up water onto his face.

"Shh, I'm sorry, *Chocolat*. It's all right. But we must be clean, eh? Truly *clean*. Now, let's have a go at those feet of yours, because they are a disgrace."

Brother Robert took Beck's right ankle and lifted the whole leg free of the water. His grip was surprisingly strong: Beck could see the muscles working in the pale arm. The priest's soaped fingers worked the boy's foot in detail.

"You'll know," he said, "the story of how Jesus washed the feet of his disciples. The Gospel of Saint John, Chapter Thirteen. Christ knew that his crucifixion was imminent." Brother Robert's fingers probed between Beck's toes, causing spasms of feeling in Beck's midsection. He tried to pull away but could not free himself from the iron grip. "Before the Last Supper, Our Lord removed his outer garments — as we have done, *Chocolat* — and washed his disciples' feet. Just as I am washing yours. Saint Peter was not happy with the arrangement. He said, 'Thou shalt never wash my feet.' And Jesus said, 'If I wash thee not, thou hast no part with me.' Are you listening, *Chocolat*?"

"Yes, Father. I'm clean now and the water's getting cold." He started to hoist himself out of the bath, but Brother Robert levered him back down.

"Wait. Then Peter said, 'Lord, not my feet only, but also my hands and my head.' And then Jesus told him, 'He that is washed needeth not save to wash his feet, but is clean every whit.' Do you understand what I'm telling you?"

"No, Father."

41

"You will. Get up and turn the hot tap. No, the other one. That's it. Good. Let it run."

Kneeling, Beck felt the rubbery caress of the sponge move across his shoulders and down his back. He tried to move away but the scald of the falling water meant he could not. He clenched himself, holding on to the capstan of the tap, panic rising in his gut. *Here we go,* he thought.

"Good boy. That's enough. Sit back down. Give me the other foot."

There was a transparent coating of dispersed soap on the water now. It seemed to Beck that beneath it the priest's thing was bigger than before. *A trick of the way of looking at it,* he thought, or hoped. Best to close the eyes. His left leg was lifted clear of the water. The sponge oozing over his foot, up his calf, teasing the back of the knee, the inside of his thigh.

Jesus, but his own thing was thickening. Little finger turned thumb.

He opened his eyes and tried to sit up. He could not because Brother Robert was gripping his ankle. Smiling and leaning closer. The rabbit eyes moist and pinkish.

"I would guess, my child, that it has been a long time since you were treated gently. Since you were touched with tenderness. Hmm? Believe me, I have no illusions about the kindness of orphanage nuns. And that is why, if you remember, I spoke to you when you first arrived about love. And you thought, no doubt, that it was the same old flannel priests are always giving out. But it wasn't, *Chocolat.*

42

I meant every word of it. Your past has been harsh, and your future will be hard. For reasons known only to himself, God has set you a rocky road to travel. But he is merciful. He has given you this interlude of gentleness and love here in this house. This gift to carry with you in the secrecy of your heart. Do you understand?" The priest's soapy hand massaged the boy's knee. "Don't refuse this offering, my son. Trust me."

Beck was unable any longer to ignore Brother Robert's swollen penis, because the priest had taken it in his other hand and lifted it clear of the water, its purplish glans protruding from his grasp.

"Like all God's wonders, *Chocolat,* the male organ is most ingeniously designed for its primary purpose, which is, as you may or may not know, the impregnation of the human female. But there are those of us, like myself and my fellow brethren, who have denied ourselves the so-called pleasures of fornication in order to serve his greater purpose. Although we do not complain of it, self-denial is hard. Even the saints struggled with carnal desire. Knowing this, as he knows all things, God in his merciful wisdom has decreed that this unruly prong of flesh also fits perfectly into the human hand. Like this. Do you see?"

Beck saw, indeed. And knew that seeing was not going to be enough.

"Take me in your hand, *Chocolat,* and wash me. As I washed you, dear child. Tenderly."

Beck hesitated.

"Do it," Brother Robert said, urgently, swimming his own hand between Beck's legs.

Silently, with a sudden lunge, Beck seized the soap dish.

Brothers Michaelis and Duncan sat on stools (stools stored away in the linen cupboard normally, but handy when baptisms were taking place) on the other side of the bathroom door, listening intently. It was regrettable that the heavy thickness of the door reduced the sounds from inside to muffled murmurings and splashes, but both men were adept at translating these into delicious imaginings. So when the extraordinary sound—somehow both a bellow and a howl—came from within, they were extremely startled.

Both leaped to their feet, Brother Duncan losing his balance in the process and half falling against the wall. Brother Michaelis fumbled urgently with the key to the bathroom door and, pushing it open, was confronted by Beck, who was naked, wet, and apparently possessed. The boy was shaking from head to foot, his teeth set in a snarl. His right hand was raised in a threatening gesture; it gripped something sharp edged and bloody.

In this frozen, almost hallucinatory, moment Brother Michaelis now saw Brother Robert half-risen from the bath, supporting himself with one hand on its rim and his other hand raised in a gory benediction. The left side of his face was masked with blood issuing from a gash on his forehead.

The moment convulsed: Beck let fall the thing he had

been holding—which was, Brother Michaelis now realized, a jagged half of the soap dish—and hurled himself toward the door. Brother Michaelis blocked him, enfolding the boy in a slithery embrace. Now Brother Duncan pushed into the room, and between them the two priests managed to force Beck to his knees and get a grip on his arms. The boy roared obscenities.

Brother Robert, his detumescent organ dangling, climbed unsteadily from the bath and pressed a towel to his face.

"Dear God," Brother Duncan cried. "What happened, Bob?"

"The savage little bastard tried to kill me." He took the towel away from his face and studied it. "Take him downstairs. I'll be five minutes."

With difficulty, Brothers Michaelis and Duncan strait-jacketed the boy in a bath towel and dragged the howling Beck down the corridor. Brother John appeared at the turn of the stairs.

"What on earth is going on?"

Instead of answering, Brother Michaelis balled his handkerchief and shoved it deep into Beck's mouth. He made an upward gesture with his head to where pale faces peered through the balusters.

"Go to bed," Brother John shouted. "All of you! Now! And stay there!"

*　*　*

The cellar was a large space divided in two by a rough wooden partition with an unglazed door set into it. Beck, choking, half-strangulated and gasping silent curses, tried to brace his foot against the jamb but Brother Michaelis expertly kicked the boy's ankle and shoved him through. It was pitch-dark inside the room; then came the rasp of a match.

"Hurry up, John," Beck heard Brother Michaelis say. "We can't hold the little feck much longer."

A soft yellow flare of lamplight. Furniture. Paintings of flesh on the walls. A cast-iron bed with a stained mattress onto which he was flung. The towel was pulled away. He twisted, flailing and kicking, unable to breathe or make a sound. His fist made contact with something yielding before it was seized and his arm yanked forward. Something metallic closed upon his wrist, hurting the bone. A great weight settled upon his legs, immobilizing them. Now his other arm was wrenched and fastened. He was facedown on the mattress snorting great gulps of air through his nose like an animal. All he could think of now was that he needed air. He turned his head, panicking for breath. The musty stink leaked slowly into his gasping lungs; terror and suffocation stifled him.

Brother Michaelis lowered his bulk onto a couch and wiped his face with a handkerchief. "Mary and Joseph, but the little shit has the devil's strength. Sit where you are, John, while Duncan fastens the feet. That's it. Now, isn't that a picture? I'd say we deserved a snifter for our trouble. Duncan?"

Beck heard glasses clink and a cork pulled. He lost consciousness like falling into a hole then pulled himself up out of it. Brother Michaelis was standing over him with a glass in his hand and a regretful expression on his face.

"Well, *Chocolat*, you had me fooled and no mistake. You led my soft heart astray, so you did. Had me thinking you were an angel with a dirty face. Bit of a wash and brushup, you'd be one of the saved. But I was wrong, wasn't I?"

He took a pull on his whiskey. "Let me tell you how it is, now. The path between the womb and the grave is a long and winding one, and uphill and hard underfoot most of the traipse." He paused to let Beck's desperate heaving gasps subside. "And on this arduous journey, what sustains the pure in heart is the gift of love. And what sustains wicked little fecks like you is punishment. We offer both options here, and you chose the latter. So be it."

The door opened and closed and a bolt slid into place.

Brother John's voice said, "How are you, Bob?"

There was no reply.

Brother Robert came into Beck's sidelong view. He wore a bandage knotted on his forehead and a fancy dressing gown. He held a bamboo cane in his hand.

The first slash of the cane brought pain so extreme that Beck would have been unable to make a sound even if he hadn't a handkerchief jammed halfway down his throat. He felt he'd been cut in half below the shoulder blades. It was almost as if it was happening to someone else in a dream of burning. During the pause between that first explosion of agony and the next he tried to gurgle a defiant obscenity, but could not. Then he burrowed down into a deep and familiar dark cave where he could not be reached.

Brother Robert lashed Beck four times on the back and twice on the buttocks. Then, his face striped tigerish by blood and sweat, he raped the boy.

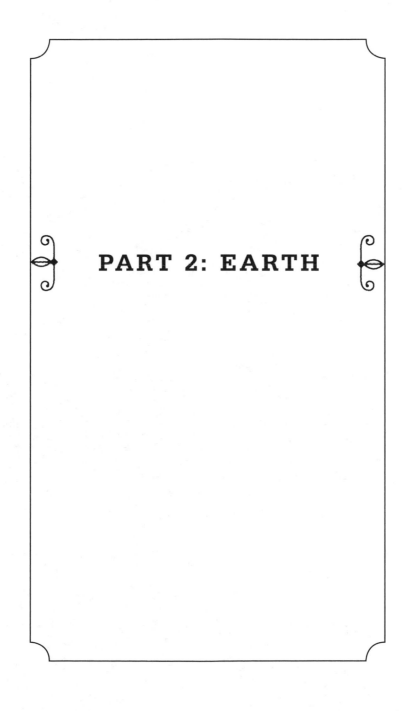

PART 2: EARTH

8

MR. GIGGS

ASHVALE, ONTARIO, HAD exactly twice as many buildings as it had letters in its name. Of these buildings,
only two were worthy of mention: the Ashvale Emporium,
a store that on its ground floor sold everything a decent
person could want. Its upper floor comprised the Ashvale
Hotel, four meagerly furnished rooms that were seldom
occupied simultaneously. No alcohol was available on the
premises. The other building of note was the reason the
hamlet needed a name in the first place: the railway station, which consisted of a single timber platform and a
low clapboard building coated in many flaked thicknesses
of white paint. The larger of the two rooms in this modest edifice was the waiting room. The other was three
offices in one: the ticket office, the stationmaster's office,
and the telegraph office, where one of Ashvale's two tele-
phones was located. This was the domain of Mr. Hicks,
who—unsurprisingly, considering his three official roles—

was an officious little man with an officious little mustache.

Twice a week, shortly after two o'clock in the afternoon and whatever the weather, an air of expectancy gathered in Ashvale. Horse-drawn wagons and even an automobile or two came in from the outlying farms and parked in the space between the station and the Emporium. The store would do a brisk—by its own standards—trade in soda pop (summer) and hot potatoes (winter). Women—neighbors separated by ten miles or so—exchanged news and recipes. Men exchanged glances. Pocket watches were studied, their reliability debated. A train was due.

And here, at last, it came, sounding its steam whistle, from the unreclaimed woodland to the northeast. Chugging smoke into the virginal spring sky. Approaching the station platform onto which now thronged the populace of Ashvale and thereabouts. Some of these people were there for a purpose: to greet a returning relative, perhaps, or take delivery of some long-awaited piece of agricultural equipment. Others were there merely to speculate: about the business of the rare stranger, or what fool had ordered a bicycle. Others—the majority, perhaps—came for nothing more than reassurance. To be reminded by the gasping locomotive that they were connected to other places, that there was—in theory, at least—something beyond what they could see.

On this particular early afternoon, the guard pulled open the doors of the goods van and produced, first, a bundle of mail and packages, which he handed to Mr. Hicks. Then a slatted crate containing a pair of ruffled and irate geese, several boxes and sacks for the Emporium, a gearbox for a John Deere tractor, two sets of automobile tires, a large mirror in an ornate black frame (this attracted considerable interest), two very big, round-bellied glass bottles wearing jackets of woven straw, a repaired saddle, a large package wrapped in sacking, and a butter churn.

From the second of the two passenger carriages, a black-clad woman stepped onto the platform to be greeted silently by her husband and boisterously by her young daughter. A man unused to the suit he was wearing climbed aboard without farewell.

When all this was done, Stationmaster Hicks consulted the fat watch chained to his waistcoat for a good many seconds then blew the whistle he held between his officious lips and raised his arm. The engineer withdrew his head into the cab with a laconic wave.

Within half an hour of the train's departure all trace of its visit had vanished. Hicks had distributed letters and packets from the glass window of his ticket office, all cargo had been claimed, all spectators dispersed, and Ashvale, exhausted by the thrill of it all, had resumed its normal torpor. There remained, however, a solitary figure on the platform: a dark-skinned boy dressed in a rough woolen coat standing next to a tin trunk. Several people had noted the words on the label pinned to his lapel: *Ignatius Beck. Giggs, Ashvale, Ontario.* But no one spoke to the boy and no one seemed keen to claim him.

Eventually Beck walked to the end of the platform. From that vantage point he had a view of the backyards of three mean dwellings. In the one nearest him, a woman was spreading wet bedsheets on a clothesline beside a rickety picket fence. She was the one item of human presence in a vast and empty landscape. Beck's experience of unpopulated spaces was limited to the awful and limitless ocean he'd seen from the deck of the *Duke of Argyll*. And now it seemed to him that he was at sea again, a sea solidified and dead under a hot white sky. From this landlocked deck, you could slide boys into nowhere they'd ever be found. It occurred to Beck that this was indeed what had been done to him.

Sweat had awakened the wounds on his back. He took off his coat, dumped it on the trunk, and unbuttoned the itchy gray cardigan. He walked to the open window of the white wooden building. Inside, the man with the cap and mustache was sitting at a desk making notes in a thick ledger.

Beck said (his voice uncertain because it hadn't been much used in two days), "Mister? Am I in Ashvale?"

The man, without looking up, aimed a finger skyward. Beck stepped back to see what it was aimed at. Which was a black and white stamped metal sign nailed to the gable of the shack.

"Fook you, then."

"You're welcome."

Beck walked back to his trunk. No, not his. The one those bastid Brothers had given him 'cause it was heavy and awkward and a sod to lug. He sat down on it, wincing.

Because there was no other moving thing to look at, he watched a heat-shivered shape get bigger as it came and went between the low swells of the land. Gradually it became a horse-drawn buggy with legs moving in unhurried rhythm. The driver's eyes blazed light when he moved his head. With implacable slowness, the vehicle approached the station, where it halted. The horse shook its head and whiffled. A minute later the driver came up the ramp onto the platform and went to the office and spoke into its window. While so doing, he took off his spectacles to clean them with a gray handkerchief. In response to something Hicks said he put his glasses back on and looked in Beck's direction. He turned back to the window and spoke again. Then he walked along to Beck. There was a hitch in his stride, as though a boot nail were troubling his foot. He stooped and peered at the label on Beck's coat.

Then he stepped away, pushed his sweat-stained hat farther back on his head, and said, "Hell's bloody teeth."

For several moments he stood with his hands on his hips, gazing about like someone seeking the perpetrator of a practical joke. Then he returned to the telegraph office, yanked the door open, and went inside. He and Hicks exchanged words that Beck could not make out. After a long silence, the man's voice started up again, growing loud and angry, like he was having an argument, an argument with himself, because Hicks wasn't talking back.

Minutes passed at a cloud's pace. The man came back out of the office, reached into the bib pocket of his dungarees, took out tobacco and papers, rolled himself a cigarette, and lit it. He drew deeply on it a couple of times then called in Beck's direction. "You, boy! Fetch that trunk down here."

Beck took hold of one of the leather handles and hauled it, scraping, along the platform. "Are yer Mr. Giggs, then?"

"Who the hell else I'd be, boy?" Giggs sucked in smoke, nipped the cigarette out, and put the stub into his pocket. *"Damn,"* he said on the exhale. "Well, come on. *Jesus.*"

He walked away and Beck dragged his burden after him, down the ramp, through the sprung wicket gate, across the rough ground to where Giggs waited by his rig.

"Can you lift that thing?"

"Not by meself."

Giggs nodded dolefully, leaned, picked the trunk up one-handed, and swung it onto the back of the buggy. He climbed up onto the ruptured leather seat and looked down at Beck.

"Yer comin', boy, or are yer plannin' to stand there like a stump the rest o' the day?"

9
BOILED BACON

THEY DROVE FOR what seemed to Beck, who was achingly hungry and thirsty, an eternity. Through low rolling farmland, fields separated from virgin prairie by nailed timber fences or rough walls of stone, through narrow stands of trees, over creeks spanned by plank bridges that rattled the buggy and sent shots of pain across Beck's arse and back. A field of grazing, muttering sheep. Beck, entirely ignorant of animal husbandry, assumed they were the same ones that had shared his ship; he wondered, without caring much, how they'd gotten here. Now and again they passed a dirt track that met the dirt road and at each of these there was a post with a board fixed to it. Or a gallows with a board hung from it. On the boards, names: MCEWEN, SMITH, KELLERMANN, GREY. He sounded out each one silently, having nothing else to do but concentrate on his own pain and thirst.

Giggs spoke not a word during the entire journey. Beck looked at him sideways at intervals. His captor was a hat, a pair of spectacles, a stubbled jaw hinged upon a neck of reddened and ropy sinews. Once, he let the horse's leather traces rest in his lap and foraged in his bib for the half-smoked cigarette, then lit it with a match. His hands, like his throat, were made of weathered string and knobs.

When the sky at its edges was deepening into indigo and the underbellies of the clouds began to pinken, Giggs *chuck-chucked* at the horse and turned right onto a track that seemed to lead nowhere. Then they crested a slight rise and Beck beheld his new home.

It was a house not unlike those he'd glimpsed earlier: a low-slung affair hunched inside a group of trees. A black chimney pipe jutted out of the roof, leaking white smoke. A tin-roofed barn, a cluster of sheds. Approaching the place, the buggy passed a pasture in which cows grazed; they were as big as monuments. They had what looked to Beck like bags of guts dangling between their back legs. One gazed at the passing buggy, lifted its tail, and hosed shit like a comment.

Without a word from its owner, the horse halted in the yard at the rear of the house and hung its head. A welcoming committee of irritable chickens gargled and strutted, gingerly lowering their feet as if the ground might scorch. Giggs climbed down, wincing slightly when his left leg took his weight, and tethered the reins to the rail along the porch. He limped up the three steps then looked back.

"Git down. This's it."

The door opened into a kitchen: a table with three chairs, a sink below the window, a bucket below the sink, a tea chest full of firewood, a black stove like a coffin on legs. Around the stove, a three-sided clotheshorse draped with underclothes. On the stove, a metal pan with a lid that rose and fell like a dying man's chest, gasping steam that smelled of meat. Beck's stomach contracted.

Giggs crossed the kitchen to a second door that was stopped open by a stone and called, "Annie? Anne!"

A muffled reply came from the barn. Giggs went over to a Welsh dresser, took an enameled mug from a hook, and filled it with water from a tall earthenware cooler. He drained it in a single draft and wiped his mouth with the back of his hand. He looked over at Beck. "Want some?"

"Yeah." And then, "Please."

Giggs sighed as though a thirsty boy was yet another predictable obstacle on life's stony road.

Beck was swallowing, nearly choking in his anxiety to drink, when footfalls clattered and the light from the inner door faltered, interrupted by a woman hauling a heavy pail of milk followed by a child and a silence as heavy as death. He lowered his mug.

The woman wore a washed-out blue dress. Her hair hung from her head like parched grass felled by sudden rain. The child, who was perhaps five years old, female and red-haired, hid behind her mother.

"Is that him?"

"Yeah. This's what they sent us."

"It can't be, Walt."

"That's pretty much what I said when I saw him."

"They said Ignatius. There never was no nigger boy called Ignatius, surely."

"I know."

"So?"

"So soon as I clapped eyes on him, I went to Bill Hicks's office an' called them Brethren in Quebec. Cost me the best part of two dollars. Talked to that Brother Wossisface. I told him straight, Annie. That we been takin' English guttersnipes inter Canada all these years, all right, but, I said, English *nigger* guttersnipes is somethin' else. You can't start doin' that to us. This is *Canada,* not the Yoo Ess Ay."

"An' what he say to that?"

"Oh, he huffed an' puffed, said he thought we'd been told. I said the hell we'd been told. Like I'd've said yeah, that's all just fine and dandy, when we got a female child in the house? Anyways, the long an' the short of it is we get to keep him a month then if it don't work out we send him back. An' anyhow, the Brother said, physic'lly this here's the best of the bunch they had available. Most of the rest is little runts."

"An' if we send him back, who pays the fare?"

"We do."

Mrs. Giggs grieved for her luck a moment or two. Then she turned her head and said, "Elsie, go on upstairs. I'll call yer when supper's ready." The child fled. "He can't sleep in the house, Walt. I can't be doin' with that."

Giggs took his specs off and knuckled his eyes. "I know it. Where, tho?"

"I dunno. The barn, I guess, till we work somethin' out. The hayloft."

"All right."

"Walt, I can't scarcely believe this situation."

"Nope," Giggs said, and headed for the stairs while his wife went out the door, slamming it behind her.

Beck stood in the resonant silence. The savory breathing of the pan on the stove tormented him.

Giggs clomped back down with a doubled-over thin mattress under his arm, a blanket over his shoulder, and a chamber pot hanging from two fingers. "Foller me, boy," he said.

"I'm hungry," Beck said.

Giggs might have struck the boy if he'd had a hand spare.

"*Hungry? Goddamn* it, boy! We're all hungry, and some of us've done a day's work. Yer eat when we eat, if yer lucky. Now yer haul that box of yourn off the buggy and bring it over to the barn."

It was a dim building that smelled of ordure, tarred wood, and sweetly of old grass. Giggs, cursing the effort involved, carried his burden up a ladder. At its top, he slung mattress, blanket and pisspot into a low, dark space.

He turned, looked down at Beck. "I ain't bustin' a gut to get that box up here. Yer can open 'er up and carry what's in it up here yerself. When yer done, come over to the house an' sit in the kitchen an' keep yer hands to yerself. Understand?"

An hour later, Beck heard Walter and Annie Giggs kick their boots off on the porch. They came into the kitchen and pumped water into the sink and washed their hands. Giggs went into the hall and called his daughter's name. His wife removed the clotheshorse, glancing at Beck as she bundled the underclothes together and took them out into the hall. She returned and put three plates on the table. Then she went to a cupboard and rummaged out an old cracked bowl. She set it down on the table a little distance from the plates. She lifted the lid off an enameled crock and took out a loaf of bread from which she sawed three thick slabs and a thinner one.

"Take yer coat off. Hang it with the others. And wash yer hands. Use soap."

He did as he was told then watched the woman take the pan to the table and stab into it with a long two-pronged fork and lift out a rolled joint of boiled bacon strung snug into its shiny blanket of fat. She sat it on one of the plates. Beck watched its juice spread. Mrs. Giggs cut slices of meat and returned the remainder of the joint to the pan. She shared out the cut meat onto the three plates, ignoring the bowl. With a ladle she fished potatoes and bacon liquor from the pan. The bowl got a share this time. She distributed the plates to each member of her family and gestured at a low stool in the corner for Beck.

Beck walked over slowly with his bread and potatoes, intense hunger arguing with protocol. Giggs mumbled a number of words in some sort of prayer of thanks, and they all began to eat.

Beck pressed the bread into the liquid, lifted the bowl and, in the absence of utensils, drank down the broth, scrabbling around in it with his tongue for potatoes and scraps of soaked bread. He finished his meal nearly as hungry as he'd started it, the absence of fat pink meat in his bowl taunting him. He looked at the pan across the room and half rose from his chair.

Mrs. Giggs glared at him, placed the cover on the pan, and carried it away to the larder.

Later, he followed the swaying light of Walter Giggs's lantern toward the barn. From somewhere to the left, huge ominous shapes shifted and snorted. The sheer clarity and numerousness of the stars overhead appalled him.

In the darkness of the hayloft the struggle not to howl fear and rage eventually exhausted him and he fell asleep. He dreamed that Brother Robert's yellow fingernails were raking his back and woke up with straw stuck to his still-oozing wounds.

10
HOW TO USE A PITCHFORK

BECK LEARNED, IN the ensuing weeks, to loathe the Giggses' animals. They were stupid and frightening and they stank and everything depended on them. Giggs and his wife and their daughter were their servants. They worked for the animals, worried about the animals, cursed and caressed the animals and, when they talked at all, they talked about the animals.

Because he feared and hated them, Beck was no good with the pigs. The pigpen was a horror to him. On his first morning Annie Giggs, with her skinny freckled legs stuck into gum boots and her skirt hoisted into a knot, handed him a bucket of whey and slops and led him over to the pen.

"This's what yer do ever morning after the milkin', all right? Mind yer don't let 'em get ter the bucket afore yer empty it inter the trough."

She lifted the loop of rope that fastened the gate. Beck balked. The ground was churned mud and excrement. The sows were grunting hillocks of filth with slimy nose holes you could see up and jaws that looked like they could chomp your arm off. The piglets were just squealing turds on legs, and they all came splodging and whingeing fast toward Beck.

Annie Giggs dragged the gate shut and screeched, "Git yer ass over ter the trough, boy, afore they have yer over!"

He forced his feet to plodge forward, but too late. The pigs were upon him in a stinking jostle. Fear and disgust made his guts contract and he let go of the bucket and threw up. The pigs ate his vomit and the contents of the bucket with equal enthusiasm.

He clambered dizzily back over the gate and fell to his knees. When he looked up the sky was a tilting backdrop to Annie Giggs's furious face.

Then there was the teasing of milk out of the cows.

"Watch me, boy," Walter Giggs said, "and learn. You learn damn quick, 'cause this's what yer goin' ter be doin' twice a day every day of the year. Cows make milk, don't matter if it's Sunday nor Christmas. And the milk's gotta come out no matter what."

Giggs sat on the milking stool, hatless, and pressed his bony skull into the first cow's side. He took a teat in each hand, almost tenderly, and began to sing. Not sing, exactly. Moan. Groan. A throaty hum that Beck slowly recognized, that took him back to the orphanage. The cow grumbled comfortably and adjusted her vast bulk. Giggs's hands rose and fell, stroking the flaccid pink teats. Jets of milk zinged into the pail. When it was half-full, Giggs stood and slapped the beast's flank. She ambled out into the sunlight, lowing thanks.

The next cow came into position and Giggs said, "Okay. Sit down and do what I did. There ain't much of a trick ter it. Start gentle then go."

Beck's mind and his hands recoiled from the hot rubberiness of the cow's teat; every time he touched it, his brain filled with Brother Robert's floating pink thing, and he could barely bring himself to hold it without gagging. The beast's reek, the ordure encrusted on her legs, repelled him further. Her heavy and restless feet close to his own worried him. Her milk wouldn't come.

"Okay, boy. Stop. Now put yer head aginst her, like I done."

Beck had to crane his neck to do so.

"An' sing to her. They like that. Relaxes 'em."

"I can't sing."

Giggs regarded him with a narrow eye. "Whaddya mean, yer can't sing?"

"Well, I can't."

"Jesus wept. All right. Hum, then. Hum somethin'. I guess yer can goddamn *hum,* can't yer?"

So he hummed the same tune Giggs had hummed.

The Lord's my shepherd, I shall not want. The humming was similar to, but better than, weeping.

"Now, git yer finger an' thumb around a teat apiece. No, the *top* of the teat. Right. Now, squeeze firm and gentle and pull down. Like yer diddlin' yerself. I reckon that's something yer *do* know how ter do, doncha, boy?"

Beck gagged.

Four nights later, while Beck sat in the corner of the kitchen slurping beans and their stewing liquor into his mouth with a hand that was almost too sore and tired to do so, he listened to their talk.

". . . useless. I mean, what we're got landed with here's just another mouth ter feed."

"Well, I guess it's early days yet, Annie."

"That last one we had was piss-poor, but he learned ter milk a cow by now, Walt. For Chrissakes."

"Yeah, that's true."

"I just can't believe how slow he is at everythin'."

"So what yer sayin'? We pay ter send him back? Get another one?"

The scrape of cutlery on plates.

"I don't know much about darkies, Walt, but"—she shot a look at Beck crouched on his stool, face blank—"by all accounts they're stubborn as hell. It ain't so much as they can't as they *won't*. They don't wan' ter do a thing, they make out they ain't got the brains ter do it."

"I dunno, Annie. This boy, he's . . ."

"Yer bein' too soft on him, Walt. Yer know what? I bet if yer laid the whip ter him he'd be milkin' good as you 'n' me in no time at all."

A pause. "Walt?"

"Yeah. I hear yer."

When Beck's best efforts had resulted in just enough milk to cover the bottom of the pail and the cow was restless, Giggs said, "All right, boy. Leave it. Get up."

Giggs picked up the milking stool and carried it out into the yard, which was filling with early sunlight. Numberless crows were settling onto the pasture beyond.

"Sit there," Giggs said, "an' don't move."

He limped off toward the front of the farmhouse. When he was out of sight, Beck went into the barn and fetched the pitchfork, which he leaned just inside the door. He sat down again on the stool. When Giggs returned, he was carrying the horsewhip. Beck waited until he was within five yards then got to his feet and pulled his sweater, shirt, and vest up over his head in one bundled movement and tossed them aside.

Giggs halted, surprised, discomfited. "Listen, boy, I don't—"

Beck turned and gave the farmer full sight of the infected oozing welts across his back.

After a moment, Giggs said, hoarsely, "Jesus, boy. Who the hell done that ter yer?"

Beck stepped to the barn door and turned to face Giggs with the pitchfork in his hands and aimed it forward, trying very hard not to let it tremble. He said, "I've been whipped enough, mister. I'm not fookin' havin' it again. Yer try it, I'll shove this inter yer guts, so help me."

The boy and the man stood facing each other. Sounds—crow croak, a hiss through the trees, a porcine snuffle—leached into what had seemed an impenetrable silence.

"There'll be no need of that," Giggs said. "Put that thing down."

"Drop the whip, then."

Giggs puffed his cheeks out and looked over his shoulder back toward the house. He lowered the whip, let its thong trail in the dirt. "Put yer things back on. We'll try 'er again."

The next day, Beck could milk cows.

"I told yer tha's what he needed," Mrs. Giggs said to her husband.

"Yeah," he said. "Yer were right, Annie."

"Spare the rod 'n' spoil the child."

"Yep. Never a truer word spoken."

11
AN INSPECTOR CALLS

ONE DAY, A day during the thick sweltering heat of August, Beck was fetched from the kitchen garden by Annie Giggs and made to wash himself with soapy water from a bucket. Then Mrs. Giggs sat him on a chair on the porch and cut his hair with scissors and swept the cuttings off the porch with a broom. After that, and to his complete amazement, he was given clean clothes: a white collarless shirt too big for him and trousers rolled up into a thick cuff. Mrs. Giggs stood with her arms folded, looking away while he put them on, then led him into the kitchen and through it and into a room she called "the parlor." It had a window that was dimmed by the windbreak pines and contained some bits of furniture that looked like they hated people.

"Sit in that chair. And wait. There's a person comin' ter talk to yer. Don't touch nothin', 'cause if yer do, I'll know."

She went to the door, then turned back and said, "If yer say anythin' bad about us, I'll make yer life merry hell. And I mean it."

He sat for almost an hour. A fat black fly bumbled at the window, then took rest at random places where Beck thought he might have killed it if he'd had something to use for a swat.

At some point, the fly's buzz turned into something else. Something swelling as it approached. A motor car. Beck heard the chickens getting worked up. Elsie ran out to greet it. There were voices. Muffled conversation from the kitchen that went on a long time. Then the parlor door swung open.

"Well, here he is," Mrs. Giggs announced, in a poshed-up voice. "Ignatius, stand up, please. This is Mr. Shillingworth from the Home Boys' Society. He're come all this way to make sure yer bein' well looked after. He's goin' to ask some questions, and you be sure to answer them true."

She shot Beck a look to accompany this last sentence, then withdrew.

Shillingworth was a narrow and exhausted looking man who seemed to be held vertical only by the stiffness of his clothes, which comprised a starched collar, a tight tie, and a brown three-piece suit. He closed the door and creaked himself into the inhospitable chair opposite Beck. He opened a black briefcase and took from it a cardboard folder. He brought out a pair of wire-framed spectacles from an inside pocket and fumbled them onto his face.

"Ignatius Beck, born August 1907. Father unknown, mother deceased. Yes? Sisters of Mercy orphanage, Liverpool. Yes? Sponsored immigration, March of this year . . . Christian Brotherhood's receiving home, Montreal. And you've been in the care of Mr. and Mrs. Giggs for, let's see, three months or so." He looked up and removed his glasses. "So. My job, Ignatius, is to follow up on you boys. Make sure you're well placed. Looked after, and so forth. In good health, and so on. I must say that you look in peak condition. The life seems to suit you, I must say. You look very well indeed."

He smiled. Beck stared back at him hollowly through eyes sunk in a half-starved face, his skin pulled tight over the bones of his cheeks. He said nothing.

"Well, I've had a conversation with your, ah, guardians. And I have to say I was told certain things that disturbed me. That you are an unwilling worker. *Lazy* was the word used, in fact. That you are very slow to acquire even basic skills. That you need supervision for the simplest of tasks. That you seem, ah, *sullen*. The phrase Mrs. Giggs used was 'never had a word of gratitude out of the boy.'" Shillingworth leaned forward confidingly. "But there are two sides to every story, hmm? Which is why I've taken this opportunity to talk to you privately, Ignatius. Is there anything that you want to tell me?"

Beck thought for a long moment then said "I fookin' hate 'em."

Shillingworth put up a hand as if to ward off the fly that still patrolled the room. "That language will not do. This is a Christian household." He pinched his upper lip between thumb and forefinger. He reinstalled his spectacles and fished a pen from the inside pocket of his jacket. "If you have specific complaints, I am authorized to report them to the Society, whereupon appropriate action will be taken. Hmm? Do you have any specific complaints?"

"They hit me. I sleep in the barn with the animals. They don' give me enough ter eat. They hate me and I hate them."

Shillingworth stood and went to the window and gazed out with his hands clasped behind his back. "Goodness me, boy. *Hate.* I am shocked, to be frank. Shocked and disappointed. Don't you realize how lucky you are? Don't you realize how good these people are, to take a . . . a boy like you, an orphan, under their wing? To share their home with you?"

He turned. Backlit by the window, his thin ears were red.

"It seems that you have failed to grasp the fact that, unlike thousands of boys like you, you have been given an opportunity to make something of yourself. To make a *life* for yourself. Yes?"

Beck watched the fly crawl up Shillingworth's trouser leg.

"I am unsurprised that Mr. and Mrs. Giggs find it necessary to discipline you. You would seem to think it unreasonable that, in exchange for their generosity, you are

73

expected to work. To behave." He softened his tone slightly. "I have spent fifteen years with the Society, Ignatius, and during that time I have seen boys with very dim prospects grow into strong, hard-working, and respectable men. You could do likewise. But only if you mend your ways and seize the opportunity that has been given you. You are unlikely to be offered another one."

Beck looked at the floor and said nothing.

"Well," Shillingworth said. "If that's understood." He returned his folder to the briefcase and went to the door. "I shall make another visit in three months' time. I look forward to meeting a changed young man. A young man who understands the benefits of both industry and gratitude. Who recognizes the chance he has been given. Do you understand me?"

Beck said nothing. He did not look up from the floor.

When Shillingworth had driven off, Annie Giggs took Beck by the scruff of his shirt and said, or rather hissed, "See? Yer ain't got nowhere ter go. Yer ain't got no help. None of us does. So git used ter it."

12
A PARTING GIFT

O N THE FIRST day of September 1923, Brother Robert received a letter.

Dear Sirs,

    That boy you sent us by the name of Beck have run off. He stoal are money and food and some cloaths and other stuff. We have told the Polis but their is no sine of him. I have discused the matter with my wife and have decided that we do need an other boy to help about the place. If you have one that wood suit we wood be glad of it but this time we want a white Christian boy.

    Yours fathefuly,

    Walter E. Giggs

Beck had slopped the pigs and was using a stick to get their crud out of the splits in his boots when Giggs came around the corner of the house and called him over. It was the last Sunday of August, although Beck didn't know it. He had long since lost track of or interest in how the days unspooled. They were all as alike as the leaves on a tree.

Giggs was adjusting the horse's harness. He was wearing a careworn black suit and tie. His wife and daughter were sitting on the seat of the buggy. They were dressed up, too: Annie Giggs in a black bonnet and skirt, Elsie in her best frock with a black ribbon pinned onto its front.

"We got ter go ter a funeral," Giggs said. "Over ter Singleton. We'll be back 'round two or therebouts. Here's what yer do while we're gone. Yer listn'in'?"

"Yeah."

"All right. First off, fetch water from the yard pump over ter the cattle troughs. It's gonna be another hot un. Then go up the meadow we cut yesterday and rake that grass over in lines like I showed yer. Yer finish that afore we're back, yer can rest up."

Mrs. Giggs harrumphed skeptically. Her husband took a step toward Beck and softened his voice a little. "I'm leavin' yer in charge, boy. I don't like havin' ter, but I got no other choice. I'm trustin' yer. Don't yer let me down, hear? Or else."

"Aw right."

"I mean it."

"Aw right."

When the buggy was out of sight, Beck let go of the pump handle and stood motionless for quite some time, watching the crows resettle. Then he walked around to the front of the house and pulled open the screen door. As he'd expected, the wooden door was locked, as were the windows. The back door wouldn't open either but when he squinted down through the glass pane set in it, he saw that the key had been left in the lock. He picked up the chock of wood used for a doorstop and smashed the glass.

In the kitchen, Beck went straight to the larder, where on a slate shelf he found half a cooked chicken under a muslin cover like a lampshade. He tore the leg off and ate it in almost a trance of hunger, stuffing his mouth with the unfamiliar sensation of meat and chewing the ends off all the bones. Digging his fingers into the breast, he ripped off the rest of the meat and swallowed almost without tasting it in a futile attempt to fill his belly. When his shrunken stomach protested at the quantity it held, he roamed the house.

The Giggses' bedroom smelled of feet and sour flesh. He went to the girl's bedroom and sat on the bed, the softness of it entirely novel and seductive. He wiped his greasy fingers on its patchwork coverlet and continued to explore, discovering a door that opened onto a narrow stairway. He climbed up into a low, hot attic room containing a narrow iron bedstead and a chest of drawers. The bare wooden floor was carpeted with dead flies. Light burned in through a small dormer window.

This room, Beck realized, was where he would have slept if he'd been a white boy. He went to the window. Its sill was thick with crisp and black little corpses. He forced the window open and looked out. For the first time, he peered out from on high at the mean little world he had been living in. It seemed to go on forever and had nothing in it that looked like help.

He completed his survey of the farmhouse then returned to the larder, intending to polish off the remainder of the food but, standing in the doorway, changed his mind. He left the house, and went to Giggs's lean-to workshop, hoisted the tool bag, and clattered its contents onto the bench. The bag was large, made of heavy canvas with two leather handles. He found that by putting his arms through these handles he might wear the bag like a rucksack. He carried it back to the house.

The wardrobe in the Giggses' bedroom was taller than a man. It had two drawers set into its base. The upper one contained gray and frayed underthings which Beck examined with passing curiosity. The lower drawer held things he reckoned he would need. He put into the tool bag a thick pair of knitted socks, a set of long johns, a shirt, and a pair of trousers made of some stiff heavy material.

It was beneath them that he found the metal box. It had a lock but no key. Beck shook it: a heavy rattle and a whispery shifting. He put it in the bag, looked again around the room, and his eye fell upon a pair of newish-looking brown boots. Too big for him, but he figured that with the extra socks on they'd do. He put them in the bag, then returned to the workshop. He used the heavy ball-peen hammer to break the box open. The coins he put straight into his pocket. There were eleven banknotes: five- and ten-dollar bills. He took two of the tens and put them into his pocket. He thought for moment, then took two of the fives also. The remainder he put back into the box.

He returned to the house and dumped the bag on the kitchen table. Then he went upstairs and put the shattered box back where he'd found it.

Now Beck undertook a more thoughtful stock check of the larder. Two cloth packages held a round of new cheese and a slab of smoked bacon. He took both. On an eye-level shelf were ranged canned and bottled foodstuffs. Some of the cans had pictures on them which, Beck assumed, denoted their contents. Beans. Some kind of meat. Carrots. He took a meat one and weighed it in his hand. He took all the loot he reckoned he could carry and put it in the bag.

In one of the drawers in the Welsh dresser he found the can opener he'd watched the woman use and the fat-bladed knife he'd watched the man sharpen. He put them in the bag. From the hook on the back of the larder door he took one of the two ex-army water flasks Giggs carried with him when they worked the more distant fields. He filled it from the well, screwed its cap on, and slung its strap over his shoulder. He looked around the kitchen for the last time. His eye fell upon a white jug on a shelf. He took it down, stood it on a chair, urinated into it, and set it on the table.

It would be pleasing to believe that by heading west Beck was obeying that huge instinct that has made our world what it is. But not so. It was just that when he came to the road the buggy's tracks in the dust suggested it had turned left, as did a fresh and fly-thronged dollop of horse manure thirty yards in that direction. So he turned right, and right happened to be west. Even if he had known how to orient himself by the sun, it would have been of little help. The sun sat at the top of the sky and watched the boy with pitiless interest, then followed him on his slow journey toward the horizon.

13

SOMETHING LIKE AN ELEPHANT

O N HIS THIRD day, Beck came down the flank of a low hill and saw glitter beyond a file of trees. He mistook it for water, and because his flask was now empty and he was very thirsty, he descended toward it. He slid down a sudden bank on his arse through thorny bushes and a haze of flying insects and found himself on a railroad track.

He stood between two tar-weeping sleepers and thought things through. There was back and there was ahead. Trains went to places. It was easier to walk on the level. He felt a bit sick because the bacon he'd just finished off had gone as sweaty as he was. He walked on between the rails, sleeper after sleeper, each one a measurement of the distance to nowhere.

Much later, when heat shimmered the air above the metal tracks and Beck had run out of spit to moisten his lips, a curious shape materialized ahead of him. It loomed out from the birches on the right of the track. Beck approached it cautiously, keeping close to the scrub along-side the track. From fifty yards, he got a good view of it. An enormous metal tank tattooed with rivets. Standing on legs of braced timber uprights. Protruding from the tank, suspended from a metal arm, a thick, slack hose made of what looked like leather. Someone had built an elephant out here in the middle of nowhere and made a poor job of it. But maybe, Beck thought, that same someone might still be around. He stood, listening intently: nothing but the incessant throb and chirrup of insects, a sound already so familiar as to be indistinguishable from silence. He moved ahead, careful where he put his feet, scanning the shift-ing gaps between the trees. He ran out of cover just a few yards short of the elephant. The ground around it had been cleared, leaving only stumps and new growth. There was no sign or sound of anyone.

He saw now that the elephant had a tail, a steel tube that descended from its body and disappeared into the ground. And that from where its trunk joined its body there was a long streak of wet rust running down the tank, and that from the bottom of that streak there was water drip-ping and falling onto a wet patch of dirt. So he went and stood beneath the elephant's rusty belly and let the drips fall into his mouth and run over his tongue and down his throat. They were warm and tasted none too good but felt delicious. After a while he unshouldered his water bottle and held it to catch the droplets. They came at a rate of about one a second. He reckoned it would take at least the rest of the day to fill the bottle. His legs couldn't deal with the thought of it, so he heaved the tool bag off and sat with his legs on either side of the patch of wet dirt with the bottle held in front of him. It didn't work; he missed two drops out of every three.

The goddamn tank must've held more water, Beck reckoned, than he could drink in a lifetime. He cursed his frustration away and stood up, then heard it: a faint continuous noise like a whispered chuckle. It grew, very slowly, into a sound he remembered. A train. He crossed the rails and stared back down the track's long slow curve and through the heat-warped air above it and saw, where it disappeared into the farthest trees, yes, a rising drift of gray smoke.

He grabbed up the bag and worked his way back through the birches until he came to a patch of scrub tall enough to conceal him, where he hunkered down and waited. And waited. Waited much longer than seemed right. The *shloof* and clank and squeal approached, swelled, until, Beck thought, the train had to be alongside his hiding place. Why had it stopped? He was clutched by panic. He had been seen. A posse of passengers was creeping up on him right now. He got to his knees and eased leaves aside and peered out.

The train hadn't stopped. It was passing him slower than a man might walk. And it was the same train that had delivered him to Ashvale. He was sure of it. Windows of the passenger cars opened and people stuck their heads out to look ahead. A plump woman fanning herself with a newspaper. A bald man glossed with sweat. A child with red hair. Elsie! No. Older. Now the guard hopped down from his cabin at the front of the freight car and marched smartly toward the locomotive. The perspiring man called a question, testily.

"Waterin' stop," the guard said, not looking up. "Long incline ahead, and the ole girl needs a drink."

"I could use one myself," Sweaty said.

The guard overtook the train and stood on the same spot beneath the tank that Beck had occupied long minutes earlier. He made easy "come on" gestures to the driver, who was leaning out of his cab, then raised a hand. The train came to a halt in a great slumping sighing of brakes. The driver backed down the steps from his cab, then climbed a metal ladder up onto the top of the engine. The guard untethered a rope that Beck had failed to notice and swung the leather trunk on its metal arm out toward where the driver was perched. When the trunk was in position, the guard tugged on the rope and unimaginable amounts of water gouted into the thirsty machine. When it had drunk its fill, the guard swung the hose back to its original position and the driver climbed down. He and the guard set about filling and lighting their pipes. They seemed to be in no particular hurry.

Now Beck noticed that at the rear of the freight car, above its coupling, there was a small balustraded platform. It was, he figured, at about the height of his chest. Or maybe a bit higher.

The guard pulled a fob watch out of his waistcoat, studied it, patted the driver on the shoulder, and strolled back to his cabin. The locomotive snorted steam from its brakes, whuffed a great gout of smoke, sounded its whistle, and began to move. Beck waited until the freight car had passed him then broke cover and ran onto the track. The train was moving at walking pace, and Beck didn't have much trouble heaving the bag onto the platform then grabbing hold of two of its uprights. But hauling himself aboard was a different matter. He didn't have the strength, and couldn't work out how to do it.

By now the train had gathered speed and he was being dragged at a stumbling trot and the muscles of his arms felt as if they might tear apart if he didn't let go. He let loose a cry of rage and desperation and the release empowered him. Hoisting his right foot then the left onto the platform, he clung, bent double, for several yards then forced his legs to straighten and propel him headfirst over the rail.

The tool bag wasn't much of a pillow, but within ten minutes Beck's sobbing breath had found a slower rhythm and he was asleep.

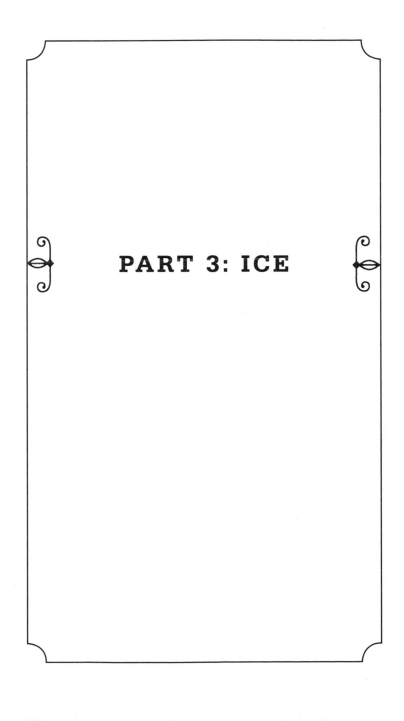

PART 3: ICE

14

WINDSOR, ONTARIO. WINTER 1924

H E HOBBLED OVER the frozen ruts of a side street and came to a stop when he saw the lights and darknesses of the waterfront separated from more distant lights and darknesses by the pallid moon-glow of a frozen river or sea. It seemed to him an impossible and unfair obstacle. He was wearing all his clothes and those he'd stolen; nevertheless, he was agonizingly cold. For a while now he had nurtured the last heat in his core like hands shielding a candle.

A covered truck passed the junction ahead of him, slowly, its lights lurching. Beck made himself walk on, passing through the mist of his breath. He crossed the road and became one of the shadows of the skeletal waterside trees. Ahead of him and to his right, sound and spilled light and the ice-silvered roofs of parked cars. He worked his way cautiously in that direction, limping quick as he could across the gaps in the trees. It looked as if there were three places where people might be eating and drinking, but there were no signs up like he'd gotten used to seeing. There was an alley that looked like it ran behind, so he recrossed the road and snuck into it. It was all iron-hard ripples of mud and snow, but when he got to the back of the first place things got slushy underfoot and there was a smell of piss. There were two garbage barrels alongside the back door and he eased the lid off the first one and was feeling around inside it when a door opened and lit him up.

The girl said, "Jesus Christ!" She was carrying a pail which she now raised up in front of her as if to protect herself.

Beck said, "Don' shout for no one. Yer all right."

"Whatcha doing?"

"Lookin for somethin' ter eat. I'm starvin'."

"You from over the river?"

"What?"

"You a Yankee?"

"No."

"You sound like one."

A gale of laughter from the open door.

She looked hard at him. "If you ain't from Detroit, what's a nigger boy like you doing skulking 'round the back a place like this?"

"Like I said, I'm real hungry."

A male voice bellowed, "Daisy! Daisy, where in hell are ya?"

"Coming," she yelled back. She emptied the bucket into the garbage barrel. "Wait here," she said. "I'll try 'n' bring you something."

"All right," Beck said.

"Don't let no one see you."

So he shrank into the deeper darkness beyond the barrels and waited, shuddering, exhaling into the ragged collar of his coat. After a very long ten minutes, he heard the door open and close and her voice.

"Boy?"

"Here," he whispered.

She came close to him. "Here."

The bowl was hot. His cold claws almost recoiled from it, but managed to lift it to his mouth. Broth with bits of meat and potatoes in it. He slurped, swallowed without chewing, felt a knotted rope of heat lower itself into his chest and belly. Almost choked on it.

"Slow up," the girl said. "Here, put this in your pocket. Keep your hands warm." She set a hot baked potato on the lid of the barrel along with a flat brown bottle. "Milk's got a shot of whiskey in, like the soup. Everything we sell here got whiskey in. Say thanks."

Beck thought if he looked at her he might cry with gratitude. "Thanks. Sorry."

From the front of the building came the sounds of car doors slamming and voices.

"I gotta go," she said.

"Wait," Beck called after her. "Yer know anywhere I can sleep?"

She paused in the doorway only to shake her head. Then she was gone.

He had a sort of rule, although he'd never expressed it to himself or anyone else. *Go on the way you're facing until you can't go no farther.* So he headed up the lane behind the speakeasies and across an open space where unguessable objects humped under the snow until he came to a dark broken wall of sheds and warehouses. He passed through the blackness between two of them and emerged onto the flagstones of a small dock. The moon was high now and full faced, surprised looking. A slipway to his left ramped down into the ice, which was scarred by tire tracks curving away toward the river. Everything was gray-blue or silver or black. Black ribs of a boat's ruins jutting from the crust. Slate-colored buildings on the other side of the dock, thirty yards away, wearing fringed shawls of ice. He felt for the potato in his pocket through hands wrapped in rags. Still warm, but not for long. The silver wind that bladed down from Lake St. Clair would kill him in the night if he let it.

The doors he tried were all padlocked or bolted from inside. He returned to the backs of the buildings. In the lee of the wind the desire to give up, to curl into himself and decline the endless succession of tomorrows, was very strong. The fourth place he came to was made of vertical boards of wood on top of three courses of bricks. Two of the boards threw a shadow. They'd sprung their nails. He reached into his coat and found the knife.

It took him half an hour to ease his way inside. It wasn't entirely dark. There were two panes of moonlight in the roof, and after a few minutes his eyes adapted. The absence of wind was almost like warmth. Much of the shed was occupied by a truck with a tarpaulin stretched over its load. Its nose, swathed in blankets, pointed at the double doors. The truck's tarp was tied tight to cleats down its sides, but at the back was unfastened. Beck lifted it and reached in. His hands found stacked boxes and explored a space just about big enough. He went to the truck's hood and lifted a blanket off it. It was cold and stiff and he put it on the floor and trod on it to loosen it up before climbing into the back of the truck and making his nest. He felt for and unstoppered the bottle the girl had given him and drank some of the milk. It still had a memory of warmth, and the smoky sweet taste of the whiskey burned pleasantly on the way down. He thought about the potato, but there was always tomorrow's hunger so he saved it. He might have blessed his luck if he hadn't long since stopped thinking in those terms.

Beck had acquired the trick of leaving his ears awake while he slept, so he heard the men's voices before the slither of the chain and the shed doors being dragged open.

His instinct, as always, was to make a run for it, but he

couldn't remember the dimensions of the space or be sure that his legs would work. He lay still.

"Jeez, Bone. It's colder'n a nipple on a witch's tit."

"Sure is. Good for the ice, though."

"Yeah. Man, you wouldn't wanna break through it tonight."

Beck lifted his head. The faintest irregular line of light along the edge of the tarp.

"You reckon our friends gonna cut up rough, seeing we're a dozen cases short of the load?"

"Nah." The voice was deeper than the other one. "They know we do the business. This'll be, what, fifteen, sixteen, runs we done this season? They'll know we'll make it up. I'm burned up with Freddie, though." He paused. "Things tight back there?"

"Hang on. My fingers're too cold to work. God, there's gotta be an easier way to make a living."

The man called Bone laughed and said, "You find out what that might be, you let me know."

Unseen hands tethered the tarp inches from Beck's feet.

"You checked the tire chains?"

"Yeah, they're fine."

"Okay. Crank her up."

The truck fired up, shuddered. A reek of exhaust. Door slam. The truck moved forward, turned, tilted, turned again. Beck got to his knees and felt for his knife, thinking to try to slice through the tarp. Then the truck slewed, throwing him sideways and clunking his head on the boards. By the time he'd steadied and readied himself, the vehicle had gained speed. Beck had jumped from moving trains and it hadn't done him any good at all. So he braced his back against the rattling cases, held on to his knife, swallowed his fear down, and waited to be discovered.

15
WELCOME TO THE USA

THE DRIVER WAS a heavyset man called Dexter Wishbone, who hunched over the wheel studying the ice ahead where it came and went between the wind-whipped wraiths of snow powder. His partner was Lonnie Smith, who tonight was not much more than a mauve beak poking out between his muffler and his fur-lined trapper's cap. Lonnie felt the cold more than most. He was a fair-weather rumrunner, Bone liked to say.

The truck jolted on a rut and lost traction for a second. Lonnie cursed and grabbed onto the dashboard. Bone turned the wheel into the skid, easing the truck back on course. It was some comfort to Lonnie that Bone was good at his job.

"You okay, man?"

"Yeah," Lonnie said. "Just be glad to get this done."

Bone grinned. "Uh-huh. I'd say you got a little bit juiced last night."

"I guess so. Don't remember a thing about it. Did I make a fool of myself?"

"No more'n usual."

The two men worked for Lew Weinstock, who was, Bone reckoned, the most easygoing bootlegger he'd ever met. And smart, too. Lew made plenty of money by keeping his operation modest, not attracting particular attention from the guys on the rough side of things. The way the operation worked was simple. Lew's younger brother, Freddie, fronted a legit but phony company called Canada-Cuba Export. Freddie bought whiskey direct and wholesale from the Hiram Walker distillery. Good stuff, not moonshine. It was illegal to consume alcohol in Canada, but perfectly legal to produce it and export it, a half-arsed, crime-loving arrangement that amused Bone. Freddie would fill in forms affirming that the whiskey was being shipped to Havana but truck it to Lew's warehouse in Windsor. Then one of Lew's teams would take it across the Detroit River to the hooch-hungry USA, making double the price.

For the parts of the year when the Detroit River was ice-free, they'd use Lew's scruffy-looking but powerful fishing boat. In the winter, they drove the cargo across the ice. Lew preferred to cross farther up the river than most other boot-leggers, past the eastern tip of Belle Isle, which meant the trip was longer and the guys had to be patient waiting for the ice to get thick enough. But that was smart, too. Because farther down, closer to the city of Detroit, the illegal traffic across the river was so heavy, they needed a cop on the invisible border controlling it. Bad things could happen down there, too. Sometimes the Yank cops backtracked on a deal or needed a favorable newspaper headline, busting a whole bunch of runners on a single night and locking them up stateside. Also, there were hijacks, gunfights, and vicious turf wars because the Mob operated down there. One night, a couple of years ago, Bone had halted a loaded-up sedan and watched four guys shoot the hell out of a car ahead of him, then torch it. He'd turned and gone back, trying not to imagine the poor dead son of a bitch driver in his burned-out husk of a machine dropping through the black cold hole he'd melted in the ice. That was exactly the kind of thing that was unlikely to happen, working for Lew.

All the same, Bone and Lonnie both had a handgun inside their coats, and a shotgun lay along the top of the truck's seat.

The guys waiting on the other side were okay. Gus and Cole. Word was, they supplied Al Capone's mob, but at arm's length. No trouble at all. They off-loaded, paid up, went on their way. So far, no trouble with the cops on their side, either. Bone figured the guys had an arrangement, but knew better than to ask what it was.

So Lew had done all right, on the quiet. He owned two boardinghouses in East Windsor, one of which Bone and his girlfriend, Irma, lived in, as did Lonnie. Irma managed the place. The other was a brothel, but nice. Lew also owned, under another name, the Majestic Hotel. Plus two speakeasies. He had the cops in his pocket but didn't let it bulge. They'd eat and drink for free but knew not to make a show of it. When they were short, he'd make them loans but not hurry about calling them in. Lew was smooth and Bone liked working for him.

Lew's brother, Freddie, was a different thing altogether. Freddie liked to dress up in a white suit and go to clubs where women were men and the other way around and cocktails were served in teacups with saucers and girls who were boys danced on the tables. And he was skimming deals. Which was why they were twelve cases short tonight. The little shit. Bone knew, they all knew, that it was so. But Lew would shrug and smile and say, "Ah, well, Freddie. He was born ass first, you know? Didn't breathe for a whole minute. It don't cost us much to cut him some slack."

Lonnie said, pointing, "Them's their lights, there, see 'em? I reckon we're off a little."

"Yeah, I got it."

Bone dropped a gear and eased the skittish truck into a curve that slowly took them between two frozen-up scows and onto a narrow dock. He came to a stop alongside a quay from which two flashlights beamed down.

Lonnie climbed out and looked up at the dazzle. "Hey, Cole. That you?"

"Well, hello, Santa Claus. What ya brought us on your sleigh tonight?"

"Most of what you ordered."

The lights came halfway down the steps.

"Whaddya mean, most?"

Bone turned his own flashlight on and said, "We're twelve units short."

"Aw, man. Ya start short-changin' us, we're gonna have to shoot ya."

"Yeah. You guys just natural-born killers. We'll make it up next run. You got my personal word on that. Now get your sorry asses down here. It's kinda cold for polite conversation."

Two heavily swaddled figures descended onto the ice and followed yellow ellipses of light over the blue ice to the truck. "Bone, my man. How ya doin'?"

"Pretty good, Gus, considering. You?"

"Yeah. You brung us kosher again?"

"Yep. Personally bottled by Mr. Walker himself. Seals unbroken, guaranteed."

"Good man. Our clients—"

A yell from behind them. "What the *fuck*! Bone, Gus! Get back here!"

Cole was standing six feet from the back of the truck, aiming the beam of his flashlight into it. Lonnie had his gun out, pointing it in the same direction.

The kid had frosted hair sticking out from an unraveling woolen cap and eyes like green china marbles. He held a knife out in front of him like it might tell him where to go.

He said, "Don't shoot me. I ain't took nothing."

"What the hell you doing in the back of our truck?"

The kid looked into the black pupil of Lonnie's gun.

"I was freezin' and just needed someplace warm to kip. Please don't shoot me."

"Maybe we will; maybe we won't," Cole said matter-of-factly. "Either way, that blade of yours ain't gonna help nothing. So why don't ya toss it real gentle near my feet?"

The boy hesitated, then did so. Bone stooped and put the knife in his pocket. "Now get out here. Slow. Try and run, my friend here'll put a bullet in you before you've gone a yard."

Beck did as he was told. He stood shaking and dazzled in the light and saw for the first time that the biggest of the men had skin the same color as his own. This might be a good thing. Or not.

Gus said, "Ya know this boy, Bone?"

"Why the hell should I?" To Beck, Bone said, "You got a funny way of talking, kid. Where you from?"

It was a question Beck found difficult to answer at the best of times. Eventually he said, "Liverpool."

Bone cocked his head like a man trying to identify a birdcall. "Liverpool? Liverpool, *England*?"

"Yeah."

Cole said, "Guys, we gonna stand here all night? I'm already froze up to my nuts. Let's either shoot the little bastard or run him off and get the job done. Bone?"

Bone shook his head and passed his gloved fingers over his mouth. Then he stepped up, grabbed the boy by the coat collar, and led him a few paces away from the truck. He said, quietly, "You're in the USA, now. Is that where you wanna be?"

Beck was so cold he couldn't think over the ice in his blood and the chattering of his teeth. "I dunno. Don't think so."

"Nor do I. So you just walk back the way we come." He aimed his flashlight back out toward the river beyond the black hulks of the scows. "Keep going till you see a bunch of lights over to your right and head for those. Understand? It's that or get shot. You got yourself mixed up in some business you'll wish you didn't."

"I didn't do nothing."

"I know. Now get going. And keep going even if you think you can't."

Bone watched the boy hunch into himself and head out into the blue-black night beneath the splendid indifference of the stars.

Lonnie said, "Bone?"

Bone turned and reached into the truck. "Let's get on with it," he said.

The runners got their usual transfer system going. Lonnie shunted cases of whiskey to the back of the truck, Bone and Cole carried them up to the quay, Gus loaded them into the back of the Americans' curtained hearse. Gus made his usual lame jokes about "the spirits of the departed."

When Bone was taking his third case from the truck, Lonnie said, "He'll be dead afore he's halfway across. You know that, Bone."

Bone said nothing.

The business completed, the money paid, hands shaken, Bone performed the tricky maneuver of turning the truck in the confines of the dock, then headed out onto the river. The full moon and the pallor of the ice meant that headlights were unnecessary, which was a good thing. Bone wound down his ice-spangled window. Lonnie glanced across at him and then cranked his window down, too.

A while later Lonnie said, "There he is."

The kid was an irregular shape that seemed to be afloat because its lower part was lost in frosted spindrift. He must have heard the approaching motor below the whine of the wind but neither stopped nor turned his head until Bone had halted the truck and stepped down from the cab.

Bone walked across the ice and took the boy by the arm. *Jesus,* he thought. *We might have left this too late.* The kid's face and lips were gray, and the snot below his nose had frozen into a brittle mustache. His eyes had a far-off unfocused look that Bone had seen once or twice before.

"C'mon, son. C'mon. Make them legs move."

After a couple of paces the boy folded in the middle. Bone scooped him up and carried him over to the truck. For a kid his size, he wasn't as heavy as he should have been. Lonnie lifted the tarp and was shaking out the blanket the kid had dragged in there with him. Together, the two men wrapped the boy up, lugged him over the boards, and propped him up against the back of the cab.

Lonnie produced a hip flask out of a deep pocket. "Reckon he could use a shot, Bone?"

Bone shook his head. "Just as likely to choke on it. Kid? Kid, listen up. You're gonna be okay, right? You just stay there and stay awake. Keep wriggling your toes, you hear me? Else you might lose one or two."

The boy moved his lips silently.

"Shit," Bone said. "Okay, let's get going."

16
AN ANGEL

THE HOUSE WAS locked when they got there. Lonnie, cursing softly, fumbled for his key while Bone stood on the step with the boy in his arms. Inside, Bone said, "Go on up. Me and Irma'll take care of it."

"She might play hell."

"She might."

"Okay. Good luck."

Bone reached out under his burden's knees and opened his door and closed it behind him with his foot. "Irma? Irma, you awake?"

"Yeah, hon. You okay? How'd it go?"

"Get in here, baby. I got a problem."

"Bone? What?"

"Just get in here, Irma."

Something deep and still alive inside Beck made him open his eyes. He saw that he was hanging above a field of flowers. No, a small garden of roses set in the middle of scuffed floorboards. Heat from somewhere. A wall with a gap in it, which was suddenly and magically filled by an angel. An angel with dark skin wearing a white robe and a man's heavy cardigan. This and all else he could see was bleared with colors coming through the heavy pearls that weighted his eyelids and a brain replaced by a block of ice.

The angel said, "In the name of God, Bone, what you got there?"

"Don't ask questions, honey. Just go and run a bath. Warm, not hot."

The angel disappeared.

Beck tugged words up into his throat. "No bath."

The face above him was all wet nostrils and mouth. The mouth said, "You're half-froze to death, kid. Plus, you stink like a road-killed skunk. You're gonna take a bath and sleep in a warm place. If you don't like the sound a that, I can always put you back out on the street."

Beck tried to shake his head. It hurt and he stopped.

"No? Okay. Let's go, then."

Waking was like rising up through deep, deep water. He could almost see himself doing it. He didn't want it to stop in case the light waiting above him was a trick—not white sky but ice. Someone was singing, either quietly or far away. He was weighed down by a heavy softness, engulfed in a cloud. It was warm. He opened his eyes, but what he saw had no meaning. The singing came closer, then stopped. He turned his head.

"Well, hello there. I thought you were planning to sleep the week out."

It was the angel he'd dreamed. Skin like the gloss on a conker, red lips, sleek short hair that came to points near her cheekbones. Eyes black as the water he'd risen through.

"Lie still. I'll fetch you some tea."

Light came through a window covered in frost. No, a see-through cloth like frost. He was on a bed. Aches came awake in distant parts of his body; they flared when he moved.

"Here. Reckon you can sit up? Attaboy. That's good. Now, drink some of this. I'll hold the cup."

Sweet heat in his mouth and gullet. The picture of a girl in his head, a bowl of soup, the smell of piss. He coughed and the angel moved the cup away from his mouth.

"Easy up, kid. Okay? Some more?"

He nodded. He drank half the cup.

"Enough?"

"Yeah." He paused. "Thank you."

"Mmm-hmm. So you got manners, leastways." She perched herself on the arm of the couch close to his feet. "Bone says you're from England, that right?"

"Yeah."

"But he don't know your name."

"It's Beck."

She smiled. The smile took up most of the lower half of her face. "It ought to be Lazarus."

"No, it's Beck."

She laughed. "Okay, Beck. I'm Irma."

"Thank you. For letting me . . ." He wanted to finish the sentence with everything. Thank you for letting me stay, for letting me eat, for letting me sleep in a warm place. Thank you for keeping me alive when I no longer had the strength to keep alive myself.

Irma was talking again. "I didn't know they had colored people in England."

He had no idea what to say. It felt like she was calling him a liar, which was something he was used to. But unused to people smiling when they said it.

"How old are you, Beck?"

"Eighteen," he lied.

"Uh-huh."

"Well," Beck said, shifting himself, hurting, "I suppose I better get going."

"You got someplace you need to be?"

He was flummoxed again.

She smiled her big smile. "Anyway, before you make a move, maybe you should take a peek under them blankets."

Beck did so. He was naked. Ashamed. "Where's my clothes?"

"Burned."

"What?"

"Bone took them out into the yard this morning and

burned them. He said they were barely good enough to use for fuel. Which was the truth."

He stared at her.

"So you just gonna stay where you are, okay? People 'round here don't take kindly to naked boys roaming the streets. Now, when'd you last eat? You reckon you could handle some breakfast?"

They heard Bone come in the street door and huff his breath, heard him stomp the snow off his boots. She'd lit the lamps and fed the stove and touched up her lipstick in front of the oval mirror, and Beck had watched, spellbound.

Bone came into the room like a brown leather bear trailing cold. He had a fat bundle, a parcel tied with string, under one arm and a smaller one in his hand. Irma kissed him, standing up on her toes. Beck had never seen such a thing happen. Two people looking at each other like it could help, somehow.

"How you doing, kid?"

"His name's Beck."

"Yeah? How you doing, Beck?"

"Okay. Thank you, mister."

"Call me Bone."

"Mr. Bone."

Bone laughed. "Just plain Bone." He dropped his packages on the floor, reached into a pocket, produced Beck's knife, and cut the strings. He put the knife on the arm of the couch where Irma had sat earlier. "Now," he said, "me and Irma gonna sit in the kitchen and talk awhile. You might wanna get dressed. Not all these clothes here are new, but they're all clean." He looked at Beck. "Do you remember last night? How you got here and all?"

"Some."

"Some is good enough. Maybe we'll have us a conversation about that later. Now get yourself dressed and come on through when you're ready. Bathroom's down the hall."

Irma said, "Coffee?" She held a cup of coffee in one hand, a bottle of whiskey in the other.

Bone slung his heavy jacket onto the back of a chair and said, "You gotta ask?"

She sighed. "That boy has better manners than you."

"True."

She handed him his coffee.

"So, hon."

"So?"

"What we gonna do?"

"Jeez, Bone, the way you use *we*. You come back with a half-dead icicle of a boy and say what *we* gonna do? What next? A grizzly bear you bring in and say what *we* gonna do with this, Irma honey?"

There was probably a word for finding laughter in all kinds of trouble but Bone didn't know what it was. The word didn't matter. She had the level measure of him.

She said, "He's a nice kid. We can't exactly send him out on the ice again."

"No. That's what I thought."

She put her drinks on the table and sat down across from him. "Where'd you buy the clothes?"

He shrugged. "Mostly from the Chinese place. The underwear from Hardy's."

"Uh-huh. Bone. How much is this boy gonna end up costing us?"

Bone looked away. Shrugged. "Honey," he began, but stopped there, unsure how to continue.

Irma sipped coffee, set the cup down deliberately. "So the plan is, we dress him up and feed him up and he sleeps the night on the couch and then we send him on his way. That it?"

Bone shrugged again. "Except I doubt he's got a way to get sent on."

They heard the boy walk down the hall.

Bone said, as casually as he could, "I was thinking there's that room, the little one along from Lonnie's."

Irma raised her perfect eyebrows.

"Like," Bone said, "I can't see no one renting it before spring."

Irma frowned. "Well, the main word there is *renting*. How you reckon some skinny-assed runaway boy gonna pay rent?"

"I was figuring maybe he could work the rent."

"Work? Who for? Me? You?"

"Maybe a bit of both."

"You by any chance notice that he ain't hardly strong enough to walk, let alone work?"

"He's just starved. He'll build up."

They heard the toilet flush.

"I dunno," Irma said. "I don't see Lew going for it."

"I already talked to Lew," Bone admitted.

Irma leaned back in her chair. "You sneaky son of a bitch," she said with half a smile. "And what did Mr. Weinstock say?"

"He said to take the matter up with the house manager. Which is what I'm doing."

Irma folded her arms. "You got the wrong name, Bone. You're soft as warmed-up snow."

He grinned. "You're mixing me up with a man who ain't a ruthless criminal."

The boy appeared in the doorway and Irma looked him over.

She said, "Beck, get in here and sit down. I'm gonna cut your hair. You're living among decent criminals now."

17

HAPPINESS BEYOND THE LAW

S O BECK BECAME a part-time bootlegger and slept in his own room for the first time in his life, although not at conventional hours. Most of the work was hard and tiresome and conducted in cold and darkness—hefting cases of beer and spirits into a truck, out of a truck, into a storage place, up into a different truck. He was happy. Outside the law and inside Bone and Irma's life seemed to him the safest place he'd ever been. He learned quickly to service the moody furnace that heated the boardinghouse (a skill Bone had never mastered), to run errands for Irma and run rum for Bone. It was a miracle to him that when he was hungry, there was food, and when he was lonely, there was company.

Irma had to teach him how to eat.

"It ain't a race, Beck. Ain't no one gonna come and grab the plate off you if you don't finish inside of two minutes. So slow down. Cut a piece off with your knife. Now *chew* it. Get the flavor out of it. Good, ain't it? All these years you been bolting your food down like some kind of animal. It ain't good for your insides. Now, count to three before you scoop up some beans. And that's a fork, not a shovel. Table manners'll get you a long way in life. That's right, ain't it, Bone?"

Bone nodded sagely and looked from Irma to Beck. "It sure is. It was Irma's table manners won my heart. Until then I hadn' noticed nothin' special 'bout her at all."

Irma laughed and cuffed him on the back of his head.

On good food, proper occupation, and friendship, Beck put on two inches of height and plenty of muscle. His face began to lose the sullen haunted habit of a decade or more. In the springtime, when they ate supper out in the yard in the shade of a big old maple, Irma teased him and he laughed, and she looked from him to Bone, solemn and shocked, and said, "Well, Bone, there's a sound I was about to give up ever hearing from the boy." And then she put her arms around Beck and kissed him on the cheek and whispered in his ear that she was glad Bone hadn't thrown him back onto the lake on that frozen night all those months ago.

Beck had never spoken to people with the same color skin as his, much less lived with them as a family. There'd been dark men among the crew of the *Duke of Argyll,* but they'd spoken to each other in a language he didn't understand. No one called Irma or Bone *nigger.* Not in his hearing, anyway.

Then there was the bothersome fact that Irma was the most beautiful woman he'd ever seen, and that other people, white and black, obviously shared his opinion. The way they looked at her. The men, especially. And it didn't trouble her. She was at ease with herself in a way that he couldn't begin to imagine. They both were, her and Bone.

Beck considered that they were better at being alive than anyone he'd ever met. And as time went on, the tiniest inkling of the faintest possibility of a life that wasn't simply one hell followed by another burrowed its way deep inside his brain.

Gradually, casually, they teased Beck's story out of him. Liverpool, the orphanage, the ship, the Brethren's house in Montreal. He told them how he'd got the scar on his calf. (Caught sleeping in a barn and hadn't outrun its owner's dog.) He told them about picking beans for a dollar a day and how the burlap sacks took the skin off the backs of your fingers when they got heavy and wet. He told them about sleeping in sheds and tents with itinerant field workers who didn't speak English and stole his wages. He told them about the bearded German house painter in Toronto who'd knocked him unconscious with a Bible. He told them about the alcoholic blacksmith in Waterloo. He told them about riding trains. He confessed to his life of crime: to stealing clothes off washing lines, to sneaking into a church early one morning and pinching food piled on the altar for the harvest festival. But despite the fact that they could see for themselves, he told them nothing about the scars on his back or the events leading up to them and they didn't ask.

He also didn't tell Irma and Bone, because he had no way of telling them or recognizing the emotion, that he loved them. Instead, just as he had become used to protecting the wintering heat within himself, he now misered the cold coin of disappointment close to his heart. Because you never knew when you might need it.

He'd been in Windsor just under a year when he crossed the ice again. Lonnie had gone down with bronchitis, barking in his room like a distempered seal. Lew's other guys were busy, so on a late afternoon when the sky above the Detroit River was a huge red ripple, Bone took him down to the warehouse and set him up at shotgun as he eased the truck across the ice.

They followed the yellow smears of the headlights onto the dock on the American side of the river below Grosse Pointe. Bone gentled the brake on and got out of the cab.

"Jeezus, Bone, what keptcha? We're like halfway to being ice ourselfs, waiting here."

"Real sorry about that, Gus. Freddie's guys just dumped the load. We had to get it on the truck ourselves. Took a while."

Beck opened his door, stepped out, and found himself illuminated.

"Who's that you got with ya, Bone?"

"New boy. He's all right."

The lights came down the steps.

"I recognize that kid." Cole's voice. "The one we found in ya truck! What the hell's he doing here?"

"Lonnie's sick."

"He's workin' for ya?"

"Yeah."

"Ya kidding me." Cole crunched across the ice and shone his flashlight up and down Beck. He grunted a laugh. "So this is Lew's big idea, huh? Get himself a whole bunch of runners ya can't see in the dark. Yeah. I can see the sense in that."

Twenty minutes later, when Beck was lugging yet another case up onto the dock, Cole took Bone aside.

"A word, my man."

"What's up?"

Cole lit a cigarette, hunching away from the wind. "Things are getting rough downriver. Lew say anything to ya?"

"Nope."

"Okay. Well, the word is that Capone and the Purple Gang have done a deal. Capone has all the muscle, but them Jew boys are crazy. They don't give a shit 'bout nothin'. No respect at all. Kill anyone soon as look at 'em. So Big Al has said, 'Okay, boys, Michigan is yours east of US 31. West of it's mine. Do what you like, just don't cross the road.' Like, anything for a easy life, you know? So Al's got Chicago; the Purples got Detroit. Brought extra guys in.

And they're not interested in honest export business, Bone. The sonsabitches just cruise the waterfront and heist stuff off anybody, no matter who they're connected to. Last week, they hijacked a consignment on its way to Bugs Moran and shot the shit out of the driver, a nice guy I happen to know. No need for it. And no comeback from Bugs. He just paid the Jews for the load and said thank you very much. What does that tell ya?"

"That we get careful," Bone said. "I'll talk to Lew. You guys are okay, though?"

"I dunno."

"C'mon, Cole. You're connected, aintcha? Capone's gonna look after you."

"I dunno," Cole said, again.

"So what're you sayin'? I go to Lew and say no more shipments till things settle? You wanna cancel Wednesday?"

"No. It's not like I got some regular job to go to, Bone. But listen. Be ready when you come across, okay? You know what I mean." Cole flipped the stub of his cigarette into the blue night and jerked a thumb toward Beck. "You wanna use that kid, it's up to you. All I'm saying is I wouldn't, myself. I'd rather have someone with me knew how to use a gun. That's all I'm saying."

Bone was silent on the way back across over the ice to Windsor. Beck glanced sideways at him several times.

18

MR. SMITH & MR. WESSON

TWO DAYS LATER, over breakfast, Bone said to Irma, "Reckon you can spare Beck this morning for a coupla hours or so?"

They walked to the dock. It was a Sunday; church bells broke the thin air like glass. Bone wore a red beanie cap and carried a satchel slung over his shoulder.

Beck cranked the truck with his hands flat on the handle, like Bone had shown him—"'cause the kickback'll break your thumbs."

They drove south and east out of Windsor, the tire chains clanking on the cleared roads between the heaped-up dirty old snow.

"How old are you, Beck? No bullshit, now."

"I ain't sure. Seventeen, I think."

"Uh-huh," Bone said, mostly to himself. "Plenty old enough, I'd say." Though he didn't say for what.

* * *

Later, Bone took a left and the clanking became a slow rhythmic crunch. Most of the tracks on the surface of this road were ghosted over. After ten minutes, he pulled into an opened-out space alongside a closed-up building with a sign across its front: M PLE LEAF HUNTI G LODGE. He turned the engine off. The silence was absolute.

Bone lifted the satchel off the seat between himself and Beck. "C'mon."

They waded into the bare trees behind the building. Now and again the rigid surface of the snow gave way and they sank into it up to their knees. They came to an open space that was firm underfoot.

"This'll do," Bone said, the words a small cloud. He put the satchel down and opened it and took out two handguns.

"Smith 'n' Wesson thirty-eights," he said, holding one out to Beck. "Take it, kid."

Beck took it. He was wearing woolen gloves with the fingertips cut off but the gun felt colder and heavier than he'd expected.

"Okay," Bone said. "Don't be scared. It ain't loaded. Hold it down against your leg like I'm doing. Now lift your arm out straight in front of you."

The gun wavered in Beck's hand.

"Now clamp your other hand on your wrist, like so. Good. Hold the gun steady. That's better. The barrel is like your finger, okay? You point at what you wanna hit just like you're pointing at it with your finger. Aim at that nearest tree. Get your eye and the barrel and the tree all lined up.

Hold it, hold it. Okay, relax. Drop your arm. You're shaking, son. That 'cause you're cold or nervous?"

"Both, I reckon."

"Yeah. I'm cold, too, so listen good. I don't wanna have to repeat everything." He took the revolver from Beck's hand. "Now, this here's the safety catch. On, like this, the piece can't fire. Off, like this, we're ready to go. You remember one thing from today—always have the safety on till you're meaning to use it. Okay?"

"Okay."

Bone showed Beck how to break the gun open. Then he reached into the satchel and took out a box of cartridges. He put a single round into each revolver, closed them, and returned the gun to Beck.

"Safety on or off?"

Beck looked. "On."

"Good. Now wait there and don't do nothin'."

Bone trudged the twenty yards to the nearest larch, pulled the knitted cap from his head, and hung it on a branch stub some five feet from the ground. He trudged back again and stood behind Beck. The red cap glowed like a lamp in the black and white world.

"That's our target. Now then. Safety off, aim like I showed you. Arm out straight from the shoulder, other hand steadying your wrist. Good. Ten bucks if you put a hole in my hat."

Beck fired. The gun bucked, sending a shock through his wrist and arm like a kick from a boot. It jumped from his hand and pushed him backward on his arse in the snow. The sound of the shot was the loudest thing he'd ever heard. It seemed to stay in the air forever like something with three dimensions. Its echoes were outraged and raucous birdcall. Beck felt like someone had thrust a hand into his chest and grabbed onto his heart. He looked up at Bone's grin.

"You missed the whole tree, son. On the other hand, you just learned a coupla things it would have taken me some time to explain." He took Beck's hand and pulled him to his feet, picked up the Smith & Wesson, and wiped the snow off it with his sleeve.

"One: You pull on the trigger nice and easy. Squeeze it back like this. Not jerk on it like you just did. Jerk on it, it'll throw your aim to hell. Two: Soon as you pull the trigger, let your arm go loose. Let it soak up the recoil, okay? Gun like this'll jump up a little, but you just hang on to it. I'll show you. Watch close now." Bone raised his own gun and fired. Chips of bark exploded from the tree just above his cap. "See?"

"Yeah," Beck said. "I think so."

"Okay."

Bone filled the magazines of both guns.

On his fifth attempt, Beck hit the tree, ripping a yellow scar into it.

On the way back into Windsor, Bone said, "You done okay, kid."

There was a long pause and then Beck looked at him sideways. "You didn't hit the hat neither."

Bone shoved the truck up a gear and grinned. "You seriously think I'm gonna shoot the shit out of my own hat?"

Three weeks later Bone plucked the red cap off the branch and, whooping, stuck his finger through the hole that Beck's fourth shot had made in it. He came back to Beck and dug a ten-dollar bill out of his pocket.

"A bet's a bet. Keep the hat, too. Don't let Irma see it, though. She knit it for me, but I never liked the color."

"Thanks, Bone."

A mile down the road Bone said, "Keep the gun, too. Don't let Irma see that, neither."

19

FREDDIE'S EVENING OUT ACROSS THE RIVER

L EW WEINSTOCK'S BROTHER, Freddie, had never skimped on the headaches he contributed to the bootlegging business, so it was not entirely unexpected that it was he who brought the whole thing down.

That next spring, when the ice had broken up and was drifting downriver in a constellation of white islands, Freddie dressed up in his suit and his sable fur coat and caught the ferry across to Detroit. It had been months since he'd been over. No matter that drivers—legitimate and illegitimate—drove back and forth with casual impunity, Freddie had a mortal fear of crashing through the ice and being swallowed into the dark awfulness beneath. From the newspapers, he kept count of who hadn't made it, whose stiffened corpses had been fished out by the police. (Twenty-eight that winter, he told his brother, and who knows how many others not yet recovered.) So he'd stayed in Windsor all winter, stoking his peculiar needs, which grew more feverish with each passing week. As soon as the ferry announced its first run, he took a long bath and oiled his hair and dressed up in eager anticipation of the pleasures of his favorite Detroit club, the Blue Cockatoo.

Which is where he met Ray. He and Ray sat at adjacent tables watching the floor show. The waitress got their drinks muddled up, and in the process of sorting this out, the two got talking. Freddie was already high on highballs and cocaine. He had a tendency to get boastful in that condition and told Ray things he shouldn't have. Ray was interested as well as charming; he had an easy smile that contrasted nicely with the dark solemnity of his eyes.

So when he told Freddie that he was going on to a private party catering precisely to tastes like Freddie's and that Freddie was welcome to come along, Freddie accepted. Ray was pleased. He excused himself to check on the address.

When he came back he offered Freddie another cocktail, which Freddie refused. Ray laughed and ordered one himself, saying the night was young, and Freddie changed his mind. When he and Ray left the club he fizzed with fragmented music.

His condition altered rapidly when he arrived at the party. There were only two other guests, who, as soon as Freddie was inside the door, forced him onto a sofa. One of the young men sat beside him and held a Colt .45 against Freddie's temple. The other sat in a chair facing the sofa and aimed another .45 at Freddie's crotch. Ray made the introductions.

"These're two of my brothers. Abe and Izzy Bernstein. You might have heard of us. They call us the Purple Gang. Boys, this is Freddie Weinstock. Freddie and his brother run a nice little operation outta Windsor, and Freddie's gonna tell us all about it. That's right, ain't it, Freddie?"

Freddie made a sound, a whimper that might have passed for agreement.

"'Cause if you don't, or if you bullshit us, we'll not-quite kill you and put you in the trunk of a car and sink you in the river."

Abe ran the back of his fingers down the sleeve of Freddie's fur coat. "Nice," he said. "It'd likely weigh you down in water."

So Freddie told them everything. Where and when and how and who. Except he didn't mention a boy called Beck, because he didn't know about a boy called Beck.

At the end of it Ray said, "Okay, Freddie. Thank you very much for your candor. Now, here's how it is. You gonna keep doing that business you got with Hiram Walker. Except you gonna be working for us now. Unless you wanna get dead and we put someone else in place."

Freddie shook his head vigorously.

"Okay. That's what we thought. So . . ."

"Please don't hurt Lew," Freddie said. "I'll do anything you want. Just don't hurt Lew."

Ray frowned and cocked his head. You could almost see his brain thinking that one over.

20
THE WRONG GUYS

B ONE THROTTLED THE engine back and brought the boat out of its slow curve. It was late afternoon on a day that lacked color. The fading light was a broad swathe of translucent steel above Grosse Pointe. One of the scows had gone; the other rocked uneasily in piebald water.

The boat carried twice as much hooch as the Ford truck, so Gus and Cole usually brought two vehicles, the hearse and a closed truck with GRAND MILLS FLOUR painted on its sides. Peering ahead, Bone could make out the both of them parked up on the quay.

"Okay, Lonnie?"

Standing at the bow, Lonnie hacked out a cough and flipped his cigarette into the water. He picked up a coil of rope. "Yeah."

Bone burbled the boat into the dock. Three figures materialized out of the gloom. One of them called out. "That you? Lonnie, Bone?"

It wasn't a voice they knew. It belonged to a tall man wearing a gray hat. His hands were deep in the pockets of his overcoat. One of his companions wore a leather jacket and a woolen cap. The third man leaned against the hearse, smoking, like he didn't want to be there, or had just happened to chance upon the scene. He wore a plaid wool jacket and a flat cap.

Lonnie glanced at Bone. Bone put the lever into the neutral position and stepped out of the wheelhouse, keeping his hand on the wheel. He patted his coat pocket like someone checking his wallet was still there, and Lonnie nodded. The boat was thirty feet from the quay.

"Who's that?" Lonnie called back. "Where's Cole 'n' Gus?"

"Capone's got 'em on another run," the tall man said. "Something came up. They lent us their wagons. Everything's kosher. Bring 'er on in."

Bone stepped back into the wheelhouse. As if checking the angle of the stern he turned his head and said, low, "Beck? Stay put and keep quiet."

Beck was down in the hold, which had a gantry rigged over it. His job was to attach its hook onto the netted cases of whiskey.

Bone eased the boat alongside the dock. Lonnie lobbed the bow rope ashore and the guy in the leather jacket inexpertly looped it over a bollard. Lonnie walked to the stern. Passing the wheelhouse, he murmured, "Don't like the look of this, Bone."

"Just take it slow," Bone said.

Lonnie threw the mooring rope up from the stern, and Leather Jacket made a dog's breakfast of tying that up, too.

Bone eased the engine into a soft chug that matched the beat of Beck's heart. He left the wheelhouse and stepped up onto the quay. Grinning like a fool, he offered his hand to the tall man in the hat. "Bone. Pleased to meetcha. Don't think we've met."

The man hesitated then took his hand out of his pocket, which, Bone noted, hung heavy.

"No," the man said, taking Bone's hand like it was a slug. "We was told forty-eight cases. That right?"

"Sure is," Bone said, releasing the man's hand. "So we better get going."

The guy glanced past Bone's shoulder and nodded. The other two men stepped down onto the boat's foredeck. Lonnie stood at the stern looking at them.

Bone said, "We got a system does pretty well, okay? I work the hold, Lonnie there works the hoist, you guys load up onto the trucks. That okay with you?"

"Yeah. Except I don't do no heavy lifting. Got a bad back. I'm just along to check what comes in is what's meant to come in."

"I got no difficulty with that," Bone said. He went back down onto the boat and reversed down the short flight of steps into the hold.

Beck had eased himself into the cramped space behind the steps. He peeked anxiously at Bone from between two treads. "Bone?"

"Shush. We might be in difficulty here, son. Load your piece like I showed you and keep outta sight."

Footfalls overhead. Lonnie's voice. "We set?"

"Yeah. Let's go."

The light squeal of the winch. The hook and chain dropped into the hold. Bone attached the first load, six cases of Hiram Walker netted together.

"Take 'er up."

They worked fast, faster than Leather Jacket and Plaid Jacket could keep up with.

There were still several cases on the deck when Lonnie clicked the lock on the winch.

"Beck?" Bone whispered.

"Yeah."

"Listen up. Three guys. One in a check jacket, one in leather. And another guy up on the dock with a hat. Don't like the look of 'em. I'm gonna go up an' close the hatch but I'll leave it chocked up a ways so you can see out, okay?"

"Yeah. Bone . . . ?"

"Just keep an eye on what goes on, understand? Anything bad happens, just climb out onto the dock away from the light and run like hell. You got that?"

"Run where, Bone?"

"Any place dark and outta sight. Don't worry. We ain't going nowhere without you."

Bone put his foot on the first step up then paused and pulled the bright-red hat off Beck's head. "Gonna be fine, son. Just do what I say. Bone'll take care of business."

He climbed up out of the hold. It was almost dark now, so he went to the wheelhouse and turned on the lamp fixed to its roof. He trained it onto the quay.

"Hey!" The hatted man held his left hand up to screen the light from his face. "Turn that fuggin' thing off!"

"Not a good idea," Bone said. "Need to see what we're doing. Don't want no one falling in the river carrying Big Al's whiskey."

The man in the hat thought about it. "Okay. Let's move it. Jesus, I didn't think it'd take this long." He stepped sideways out of the light.

21

BECK MAYBE KILLS A MAN

WHEN HE HEARD Lonnie say, "That's it, fellers. Last case," Beck stood on the third step and peered out. He could see the patched-up surface of the quay, a truck with red writing on it and part of another vehicle with glass sides.

The shooting and shouting started before he had time to figure out where anyone was. Three shots then a pause no longer than a heartbeat then another shot and another. They seemed to come from all over the place; Beck's eyes registered flashes but they were as random in the dark as prairie lightning. Shaking, he took the Smith & Wesson from his pocket, slid the safety off and rested the barrel on the raised rim of the hold, trying to steady it. Then he saw Lonnie's silhouette reverse across the foredeck. Lonnie's head was back like he was screaming at heaven but his arm was pointing at the quay and his gun fired twice before his legs gave out and he fell slumped against the boat's gunwale.

From Beck's right, frighteningly close, came another bang and flash. Something heavy landed on the deck in front of the wheelhouse. Silence, then a voice he didn't recognize called out.

"Mannie?"

A reply came out of the darkness on the quay beyond the bow of the boat. "I'm hit. Jesus, I'm hit." Then a hat toppled into the light, followed by a man crawling forward like a pilgrim toward a shrine. "I'm fuggin' hit, Joe. Get that son of a bitch."

Beck caught a gleam of metal and a leather arm at the edge of the lamplight. A shape slithered along the deck toward him. Bone.

Another shot. Both side wheelhouse windows exploded into frost.

"Beck," Bone said hoarsely, on his knees now, shedding glass like a dog shaking off water.

Beck braced himself and fired into the darkness where he guessed the man in the leather jacket might be. The bark of the gun turned into the whack and whine of a ricochet. Then a yelp. "Shit, Mannie, they got someone else with 'em!"

Bone heaved himself upright and swiveled the lamp. Dazzled, the man in leather aimed blindly. Beck steadied his right wrist and shot twice. The double recoil threw him backward down the steps into the hold. He heard Bone's gun. And again. Beck scrabbled on the floor for the pistol as the hatch above him lifted.

133

"Easy, Beck. It's Bone. Come up. Crawl up to the wheelhouse. The side away from the dock. Keep your head down."

They squatted side by side. Glass crackled beneath their boots.

Bone whispered, "You done real good, son. Now listen."

Beck leaned out and looked past Bone toward the black shape near the bow. "Is Lonnie dead?"

"I reckon we got two of them guys, but one's still out there. Guy in a plaid jacket. He ain't had nothing to say so far, but I dunno where he is."

"Lonnie might be okay," Beck said.

"*Listen*. How many shots you loose off? Three?"

"Yeah."

"Okay. I'm empty. Here, reload for me. Ammo's in my pocket."

"Bone?"

"I'm hit in the arm. Can't do it myself."

"You okay, Bone?"

"Shut up, kid. Just load me."

Beck did as he was told. His jittery fingers fumbled at the third chamber and the round dropped onto the deck.

"Steady." Bone's voice was calm.

Beck handed the revolver back to Bone. The silence was dense and eerie. Ice shunted softly against the hull.

"Okay. Now listen. Stand up real easy. Get up on my back and from there onto the roof. Stay flat. Reach up and run the light real slow along the dock. Anything kick off, just hug the roof like it's your best girl and let me take care of business. You got that?"

Beck said nothing.

"Beck?"

"I need a piss, Bone."

"You piss your pants, it'll be the least worst thing happens tonight. Let's go."

Beck stood and hoisted himself up onto the wheelhouse roof. He swung the lamp. It lit up the guy in the leather jacket. He was lying flat on his back twenty feet away with his head between two metal barrels. Beck thought at first that the glistening puddle he lay in was blood, then saw that one of the barrels was punctured and leaking oil onto the corpse.

He tracked left, the beam showing up a shrouded rowboat, a marine engine sitting on blocks, the blind and stained brick wall of a warehouse, the flour truck, the hearse, and a man in a long coat lying facedown, absolutely still, his face crushed into his hat.

"Okay," Bone said, hissing relief.

Something creaked. Beck swung the lamp at the flour truck. The passenger door was part open, and a plaid arm appeared. The hand at the end of the arm was waggling a handkerchief. "Don't shoot! Don't shoot! I ain't got a gun!"

From the shadow of the wheelhouse Bone shouted, "Stay where you are." And then, quietly, "Get down here, Beck."

Beck slithered down and, at Bone's signal, climbed over the gunwale and took up a position ahead and to the right of the truck's cab. Bone climbed down onto the quay and walked toward the truck. His left arm hung limply, and now Beck saw a ragged tear in the sleeve below the shoulder. Blood dripped from Bone's fingers.

The man inside the truck called out again. "What you doing, boys?" There was a sob in the question. "Please. Don't shoot. I ain't carrying, honest to God."

"Get out," Bone ordered.

The man scrambled out with his hands high and his eyes shut. "Please," he said again.

"Take your coat off and throw it this way."

The guy did.

"Now drop your pants."

The guy opened his eyes. "What?"

"You heard me."

He was maybe fifty years old with worry dribble on his whiskery chin. He fumbled with his belt and buttons and let his trousers fall, exposing long johns that hadn't visited a laundry for some time. His eyes swiveled from Bone to Beck and back again. He began to babble. "Listen. I never meant you boys no harm. I been a boat skipper up and down Detroit for twenty years. They said it'd be all safe with no one getting hurt, least of all me—"

"Shut up."

The guy shut up.

Bone said, "You were gonna steal the boat off of us? That's what you're saying?"

The man opened his mouth but thought better of it and

shut it again. Bone stepped up to him and aimed his gun at the middle of the man's face.

"Oh, dear God, Jesus. Please. I got a wife and three kids and I didn't know nothing about this at all. It was just a job."

"I'm strongly minded to kill you anyway," Bone said.

The man was sobbing now. "Please don't. Please, please don't."

Beck was thinking the same thing.

"Get in the truck," Bone said. "No, asshole. The back of the truck. Beck, take the keys out of the ignition and lock the front doors."

The guy shuffled along moaning with Bone's gun an inch from his head.

"Get in."

He did as he was told, sitting hunched on a case of whiskey with his trousers around his ankles like a man on the toilet. Bone put his gun away, which emboldened the guy to stop sniveling and speak. "No offense, mister, but you and yon other nigger's good as dead. You just killed two of Abe Bernstein's boys. I don't think there's any way of getting on the right side of that."

Bone said, "You got problems of your own, skipper. You're gonna spend the night locked up with a load a whiskey belongs to the Purple Gang. I'd say you could really, really use a drink right now. Temptation's a terrible thing." He took the keys from Beck and closed the doors and locked them, then lobbed the keys underhand into the water. "Good luck," he called, and left.

Beck relieved himself lengthily and messily where he stood because he was unable to control his shuddering. He climbed back on the boat as it rumbled to life.

"C'mon, son," Bone called from the wheelhouse. "Let's get the hell outta here."

With Bone steering one-handed and Beck working the throttle, they maneuvered out into open water. Ahead of them, the newly risen half-moon made intermittent appearances through breaks in the running clouds. After ten minutes Bone turned the bow into the current and told Beck to idle the engine. Then, grunting a little, he shrugged off his heavy coat. In the dim light of the cabin lamp his shirtsleeve was black with blood. Bone took a jackknife from his pocket.

"Here," he said. "Cut it right up to the shoulder." He looked at Beck and managed a small smile. "And try not to shake."

Beck sawed through the cloth of the sleeve and the undershirt. Wincing, Bone peeled the sticky and stiffening fabric away from the flesh and explored his wound with the fingers of his good hand.

"Well," he said. "Got me a lucky one. Went through clean." He tapped a box with his foot. "There's oil rags in there. See if there's a couple ain't been used much."

Inexpertly, under Bone's more or less patient direction, Beck dressed the wound and helped Bone to get the parka back on. Bone gave the wheel a quarter turn and told Beck to gun the engine a quick burst. "Okay, now listen. What we gotta do next is drop Lonnie over the side."

"What? Jesus, Bone. No."

"You want me to take him back over and call a funeral parlor? Say there's a bootlegger on a boat shot to shit and would you take care of it only don't tell no one, specially the cops?"

"But . . ."

"C'mon. I can't do it myself."

It was hard for Beck to look at Lonnie, who sat in an interlude of moonlight with his eyes and mouth and coat open. His belly and lap and thighs were drenched with blood. Bone stooped and got his right hand on one of the lapels of Lonnie's coat. Beck didn't move.

"*C'mon,* kid!"

"Ain't you gonna say nothing first?"

"What?"

"You know."

Bone straightened. "Jesus Christ," he said. "Well, you know what? I can't think of a single prayer appropriate to the occasion. You?"

Beck said nothing.

"Take his legs," Bone said. And then to Lonnie, "I'm sorry, pal. I guess you'd know we got no choice."

22

BECK MAKES THINGS DIFFICULT

WHEN THEY WERE nearing the lights of Windsor, Bone said, "When you got us tied up, kid, run like hell home and tell Irma to get her ass down here. And bring the keys to the Ford, okay?"

But there was no need. The truck was waiting on the quay and Irma climbed out of it. Beck didn't recognize her at first; she was wearing a heavy jacket, trousers, and a man's cap. Beck threw her the bow rope and she looped it over a bollard, and when he jumped down from the stern she went to him and put her arms around him without saying anything. Then she saw the awkward way Bone was climbing off the boat. She ran to him. "What happened?"

"We got heisted. Lonnie's dead. I'm hit in the arm. Ain't gonna kill me. I'd kinda like one of them hugs, too. But leave my left arm out of it."

Beck stood watching them embrace. After a while Irma looked at him past Bone's shoulder. She had tears in her eyes. "You okay, Beck?"

"Yeah."

"He did well tonight," Bone said. "Real well."

Irma let go of Bone and stepped away from him and wiped her eyes on her sleeve. "Listen," she said. "Lew's dead."

"What?"

"Fran called me —"

"Who?"

"Lew's housekeeper. Said she was upstairs, heard Lew answer the door and then shooting. After a while she goes down and Lew's lying dead in the hall."

"Christ, Irma. When was this?"

"She called an hour, hour 'n' a half ago. I've been down here an age, baby, terrible things going through my head, wondering why you was so late back. Wondering if you'd come back." She was crying and angry with herself.

"Hush, honey," Bone murmured. "We're okay."

She shook her head. "It's over, Bone. We gotta get out."

"Yeah. Maybe. I'm done in, hon. Let's get back to the house and —"

"No," Irma said. "It ain't safe. Besides, we gotta get you to a hospital, fix you up."

"You crazy, Irma?"

"Doc Bergman, then."

"All right. Bergman. And hope the son of a bitch is sober."

141

Beck stood silent and watchful. He didn't understand what was happening but knew it was bad. He felt the cold hands of some implacable clock move into a darker hour.

Now Irma turned to him. "Beck, honey? Get in the truck."

Irma drove. Beck sat between them. It was a squeeze in the cab because there were two fat items of luggage on the floor and Beck and Bone had to fold up and put their feet on them. Beck closed his eyes for a minute and wondered how sitting there made him feel safe, despite everything.

"So, tell," Irma said. "What happened over there?"

Bone told her.

Twenty minutes later, Irma pulled up alongside a quiet suburban house. She left the engine running and helped Bone up to the front door, which eventually opened. Beck sat in the truck. The moon was gone and snow began to fall, fine as salt, mesmeric. Beck fell asleep.

He woke up when Irma got back in the truck and jacked the engine into gear. They drove off.

"Irma?"

She fumbled for the wiper switch. The blade staggered across the glass.

"Is Bone okay?"

"Yeah, he's gonna be fine."

"We going home?"

She didn't answer.

"Irma?"

She said, "Bags under your feet? The smaller one's yours. Got most of your stuff in it." She took her right hand from the wheel and dug out something from the pocket of her coat.

"Here. There's two hundred dollars. Divide it up, put it in different pockets, the bag, your boots. You listening? Don't ever let no one see it all at once."

Beck stared at the roll of bills. "What's it for?"

"Take it. You gonna need it."

Headlights came toward them and Irma cussed and steered over to the right. "Now," she said, "you still got that gun you think I don't know about? Well, throw it out. Black boy with a gun is a shortcut to hanging. Go on. Open the window and throw it out."

He did it. And said, "Irma? I think maybe I killed someone tonight."

She said nothing for some time. Then glanced sideways at him, reached over, and briefly gripped his hand. "You're a good boy, Beck. Don't let anyone ever tell you different."

It felt to him like she was saying good-bye.

A little later she pulled the truck into a parking lot in front of a long, low building with lights along its frontage.

"Where are we?"

"The train station," Irma said. "Now, listen, Beck. Here's what you gonna do. You gonna go in there and find the men's room, okay? Anyone try and talk to you, you just walk on by. You get into the men's room; you clean yourself up.

You got blood on your hands and the sleeves of that jacket and Lord knows where else. Anyone ask, say you work in the slaughterhouse. Then find a cubicle and change your clothes. There's fresh in the bag. Then what you do is go to the ticket office and buy a ticket on the first train outta here. Far as I recall, there's one going to Toronto in an hour or so. Get that one, unless there's one earlier."

"We're going to Toronto, Irma?"

She closed her eyes wearily. "*We* ain't going. You are."

His throat was full of ice. He had to squeeze the words through it. "I wanna stay with you and Bone."

She looked at him now. "I know you do, honey. But you can't. Those men over there tonight and the men who shot Lew gonna come looking for us. I won't have you caught up in it, Beck. It'd just bust my heart if . . ."

"I can handle myself, Irma." A sob broke in his throat.

"Go." She reached across him for the door handle. "*Go!*"

His thoughts scrambled for a handhold. "We could run off together. Like we was family. Like you and Bone was my . . ."

She rolled her eyes. "You saying I look old enough to be your mother?"

To Beck, she did.

"Enough, now. You do what I say. You put as much distance between yourself and trouble as two hundred dollars'll buy you. If you're careful, it might get you all the way to the West Coast. People say Vancouver's a good place, even for coloreds. Head for there."

144

"Please, Irma."

Her eyes were wet but she brought one hand down on the steering wheel, hard. *"Get out of the goddamn truck."*

He did, dragging the bag. She slammed the door, had driven thirty yards when he wrenched open the driver's door panting, so she had to brake. He leaned in and put his head on her lap, choking despair.

She took one hand from the wheel and hesitated before resting it on his cheek. "Lord," she said, "you sure know how to make things difficult."

"I'm scared," he said.

"That's good, Beck. Fear's what keeps you alive. Now head for Vancouver, like I told you. Who knows? Me and Bone might end up there, too."

He looked up. "You promise?"

"I can't even promise myself to stay alive right now, honey. Now git." She pushed him away. *"Git!"*

Her foot hit the gas so hard she left nothing but the smell of rubber and a hole in his heart. A howl rose up in him but he pushed it down into the same place the rest of the howls lived. And a determination formed in his head right then not to fall for the ruse of kindness again. It led to nothing but pain.

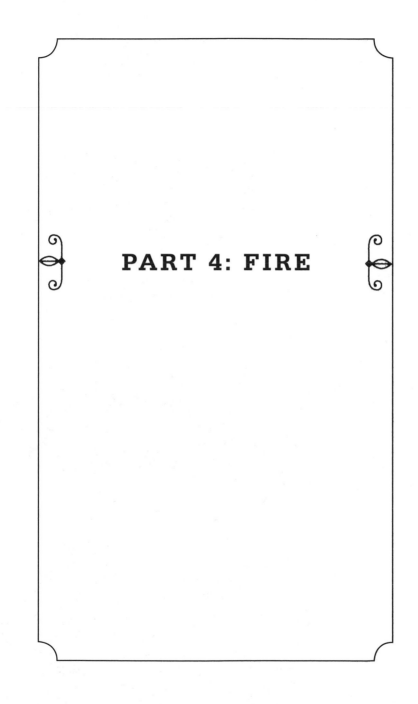

PART 4: FIRE

23

A PRAIRIE CANDLE

BECK WOULD DREAM the burning tree for the rest of his life. More often and more clearly than being robbed of his money. More often and more clearly than the hobo who'd emerged from a heap of sacks on the freight train out of Regina and said he would eat him raw.

He would dream the road, too. Tarred, shimmery, undulating, unending. Walking was like rolling it backward with his feet and staying in the same place. The same limitless field of pale-green wheat to the right of the road. The same limitless field of pale-green wheat to the left of the road. Winds making tides in both. Purple-gray mountains ahead of him, distant as heaven.

He'd been lost within himself, so when the rumble came he thought, hoped, it was a vehicle going in his direction. He turned, preparing himself to flag it down and be disappointed when it didn't stop. And saw, above the pale horizon, that the vast sky had filled with oceanic night.

Black waves, immense, capped with gray spume, collapsed and folded into each other with implacable slowness. In the darkness beneath them, forked crackles of brilliant light fingered the earth. The air groaned.

Beck stood in the narrowing space between the sunlit world ahead of him and the dark chaos behind. For a few moments, it was a kind of calm; then the wheat writhed, flattened, and hissed. A wall of wind, unstoppable and full of ice, hit him, knocking him to his hands and knees. His hat whirled away. His clothes fought to follow. He crawled off the road into the wheat, grabbed handfuls of it to tether himself to the earth, buried his face in it.

The ice hammered him for an eternity that lasted less than a minute then raced on across the prairie, hooshing through the wheat like a beaded curtain. A deluge followed: rain so heavy and thick it seemed to have no air in it. Beck was drenched in an instant. The earth in front of his face liquidized and spat at him. He forced himself, panicked, to his hands and knees, fearing he would drown. It was like kneeling in a waterfall. He lowered his head, gasping at the sparse air below his body. He endured; the rain ended as suddenly as it began.

Beck lifted his head.

The black sky had lowered itself onto the plain. There was only a narrow zone of dim green light between it and the earth. The air smelled sour and brassy like old coins. A couple of hundred yards away, Beck saw the ragged silhouette of a small stand of trees, one of those inexplicable lonely copses that serve to make the vast prairie seem vaster still and more empty. He had no idea what horrors the storm still held and doubted a bunch of trees would do much to defend him. But anything was better than lying in the open, vulnerable as a worm. As if to confirm this thought, the sky rumbled again like the warning in a dog's throat. He clambered to his feet.

He was within fifty yards of the copse when a jagged flash of light exploded just above his head, making him deaf. He lost consciousness and found it again; in the short shocked interval between the blast of light and sound he found himself sitting on his arse, bleating terror. There was a glimpse of a burning jagged break in the darkness just before the blinding light erupted again and made everything invisible. Beck threw himself forward onto the ground and hid his face in his hands, hearing, as he did, an almighty crack that faded into a loud and angry hiss. When he dared lift his face he saw that the tree nearest him, the one standing slightly apart from its fellows, had been split vertically from crown to heart and was on fire.

Because the furious light had turned his vision green, the tree seemed to Beck to be burning underwater. Too stunned to move, he watched it blossom flame, watched its burning halves slowly separate like lowered arms. He flinched at the next godclap of thunder, but it was more distant. The storm had overtaken him, traveling westward in pursuit of its angry business at a speed he envied. Behind its huge and almost straight black tail the sky resumed blueness as if nothing had happened.

He approached the stricken tree. Its twigs and smaller branches flared and crackled. Little flames, quick as lizards, ran up its black and riven trunk. The same wind that fanned the fire turned Beck's sodden clothes heavy with cold. He came within range, turned his face and chest to the heat but could not control his shivering. After a minute he unshouldered the old army rucksack and emptied the water out of his boots. He peeled his clothes off, wrapped himself in his blanket, and wrung everything out as best he could, holding his shirt spread out to the fire. Whispers of steam rose from it but he knew it would take time. So he went into the copse and gathered whatever sticks he could find, improvising a little fence close to the burning tree. On this he spread his wretched clothes, shivering as much with shock as cold.

He reached into the old rucksack. His bread was mush. He squeezed it in his hands to get most of the water out of it, turning it into a sticky ball, and ate it with a bit of cheese speckled with mold.

He stood and watched the tree burn. Now and again a flame would find a vein of sap and flare up. All the time, the tree muttered and pinged and groaned as it died. When the wind finally eased, the tree stood flickering and blackening inside its smoke. After a while, Beck lay down on his side and curled up. He slept fitfully. When he could no longer ward off consciousness he got to his feet. Part of his fence had collapsed. His clothes were warm and damp. He dropped his blanket and began straightening his fence when something made him turn. Ten yards away, standing in the wheat, a woman wearing a man's work clothes was watching him.

24

GRACE McALLISTER'S STORY

GRACE MCALLISTER WAS a troublesome woman from a long line of troublesome women. Her grandmother had been a fierce but respected speaker at the gatherings of the Siksika, Assiniboine, and Cree peoples at Saamis, which the white people translated to Medicine Hat when they took the land. She had been awarded the name Straight Speaking.

When Straight Speaking had a second daughter, she named the child Alsoomse, meaning "independent." Despite this prediction, she was outraged when Alsoomse, in 1885, aged only twenty, met and married a railroad surveyor named Donald McAllister. Straight Speaking did not attend the wedding, a meaningless ritual conducted in a tin church. A year later, McAllister was promoted and recalled to faraway Winnipeg. Straight Speaking never saw her daughter again. Alsoomse (or Alice, as she was then known) died of tuberculosis in 1904 when her daughter, Grace, was ten years old.

Outwardly, Don McAllister was a precisely rational, reserved sort of a fellow. His colleagues and even his few friends frequently used the word *dour* to describe him. In fact, he was like the locomotives he served: a logically engineered machine powered by fierce and elemental heat. McAllister's firebox was love. Amorous and unquenchable love for his wife, devoted and protective love for his child. When his work took him away from them, as it too often did, he felt their absence as a hot ache in his chest. When Alice died, this ache became a pain that he could sometimes subdue but never overcome. It etched itself into his face. By the time he was fifty he looked at least ten years older.

Stunned by grief, it took him some months to discover that his half-Siksika daughter was being tormented by the other girls at her new school. This angered and dismayed, but did not surprise, him. He had known that, behind his back, other men had referred to Alice as "McAllister's squaw." So he took Grace out of school and hired a tutor. He himself taught her mathematics, geometry, and geography. This arrangement saved him the additional pain of separation. Now, when he went on trips to inspect track laying and bridge building he took Grace with him. He persuaded himself that his reasons were educational.

McAllister had insisted that Alice teach both him and their daughter her native language. He struggled manfully to wrap his Scottish tongue around its pronunciation and master its slippery verbal constructs. Grace grew up effortlessly bilingual. After his wife's death, Don instituted the custom that at mealtimes he and Grace would speak only Siksika, even though there was no Siksika word for *fork* (when it meant an eating implement) or *dessert*. These difficulties made Grace laugh. She thought up her own words to fill the gaps.

On McAllister's visits to Canadian Pacific projects, the civil engineers, the workers, even the melancholic Chinese laborers, were amused that the stern supervisor of works always had his young daughter in tow. Over time, the way these and other men looked at her changed, and McAllister eventually noticed. At seventeen, Grace was a beauty. Her father decided it would be better not to expose her to the crude attentions of working men—and better that such men were not distracted from their work. Thereafter, when he went on tours of inspection, he reluctantly left her at home, in the charge of his cook and his housekeeper.

Don McAllister had three analgesics for the pain of bereavement: his work, in which he immersed himself obsessively; his increasingly anxious love for his daughter; and alcohol. At home, in the evenings, he drank steadily and calmly, always going up to bed before his speech and his legs failed him. In rough prairie hotels and hostelries, in canvas encampments, he would eat dinner, spend two hours writing up his reports, then crawl inside a bottle, always careful to leave a finger or two of whiskey for the morning to steady his hand when he shaved. He also smoked heavily. These habits inevitably exploded the same little genetically laid mine that had killed his father and his uncle. In March 1913, while he was struggling to open an umbrella outside his office on Portage Avenue, a blood vessel in his brain burst. Mercifully, he felt nothing when his face hit the sidewalk.

A month after his death, Grace took off the black taffeta mourning clothes and took stock.

She was eighteen years old, and an orphan. She was unmarried, though not a virgin. Several men had courted her and, despite her father's jealous watchfulness, she had been to bed with two of them.

Grace was an educated woman at a time when few Manitoban women were. After college, she studied law in the chambers of her father's solicitor, George Chapman. Several aspects of this study quietly enraged her. Her father had left her a surprising amount of money, plus valuable shares in the Canadian Pacific Railway Company. And the house.

So she was also rich.

Her wealth made her independent but also vulnerable. The second of the two men she had slept with was Chapman's son, James. He, like most men of his time and class, had assumed that by consenting to sexual intercourse she was consenting to marriage. Despite Grace's wealth, intelligence, and beauty, James also harbored a feeling that he would be doing her a favor by marrying her.

Grace did not share this view. She decided to leave Winnipeg, having come to the conclusion that her mother's tuberculosis had been a form of homesickness. Grace felt something like it herself. On trips with her father to far-off Regina or Saskatoon, she had experienced a sort of yearning in her blood, a westward pull. She did not feel at home in Winnipeg, despite never having lived elsewhere. She cared little for the opinion of society, but understood that the affliction of mixed blood meant she was barely tolerated by those possessed of racial purity. And that only on account of her fortune.

She spent a week going through her father's papers and effects, and afterward went to George Chapman's office with her instructions. The house was to be rented, with the proviso that Mary, the housekeeper, and Beth, the cook, retain their positions. Half her father's assets were to be converted to cash. Chapman was to buy back from the government two hundred and fifty acres of her mother's tribal land. She had precisely indicated the area on Don McAllister's map. She would build a house there and live in it.

Chapman was astounded and appalled. He tried in vain to dissuade her. When informed of Grace's intentions, his son went immediately to Grace to protest, only to be told by Mary that Miss McAllister was not at home. James received similar information on several further occasions and, in early July, when Grace boarded the westbound train, made a frightful exhibition of himself by falling to his knees on the platform and begging her to stay. Grace watched him slide slowly away till he was swallowed by a huff of steam.

* * *

Grace brought the hired trap to a halt. The mare stood peaceably, lazily swishing her tail at flies. She took her father's field glasses from her satchel and used them to track the line of red-striped survey poles that defined her property. It was the narrower, northern section of a low valley formed, Grace imagined, by some great geological shrug or slump a million years ago. The floor of the valley was not uniformly flat; long grassy silvery green hummocks were folded into it, separated by clumps of aspen, choke-cherry, and prickly rose. A line of cottonwoods and willows indicated the course of the creek that flowed at the foot of the valley. There was a small lake, too, according to the map, invisible from the road.

Grace lowered the glasses. In choosing her new property she had not been guided by mere sentiment. Her father had taught her that railways not only connect places; they also create them. The place they called Cooper's Creek Halt, three miles farther down the road, was at present just a refueling stop: a siding, a bunker of coal, a water tower, a pump house, and a couple of sheds. But it wouldn't stay that way. Like other once remote and nondescript way stations back east, it would grow. Grace hadn't come here to hide. She'd come to prosper. All the same, she'd hoped, believed, the valley would be beautiful. And it was. She surrendered to an immense feeling of joy.

She tethered her mare in the shade of a small bluff of birches, then set off in search of the creek, cursing her foolish city shoes. Bronze grasshoppers sparked from the grass at her approach. When she finally reached it, she was satisfied to note that it was full and steadily flowing, furling clear as glass over smooth flat stones. She threaded her way through the trees, following its course. In the shade the flies were a pestilence.

The lake immobilized her with its loveliness. It was perhaps half a mile long and not wide; a man with a good arm could throw a baseball across it. It was still as a mirror. On its far side, the wall of the valley stood in its own reflection; at its center, a single white cloud floated. Grace stepped onto the narrow silty foreshore, startling a pair of small waterfowl. They spread their wings and ran across the surface of the water, croaking outrage, then disappeared into a bed of reeds. The reflections trembled, came unspliced, regathered themselves.

It was all good, Grace thought. Very, very good. She took off her shoes and stockings and hoisted up her skirt and petticoat. The cold water on her feet and ankles thrilled her and she stripped off the rest of her clothes and waded back in. When the water reached her hips she closed her eyes. Her nakedness felt like a submission, a solitary baptism. She knelt. Coolness reached her throat. She let herself fall backward and float into the cloud.

25
OGYGIA

THE VALLEY, AS usual, had protected them from the worst of the storm but the whip in its tail had torn off, buckled, and thrown away half the tin roof of the hay barn. Grace knew that wet hay exposed to the sun had a habit of nurturing fire deep within itself, so she started up the stubborn Ford flatbed truck and set off to Jim Calf Robe's place to see if he had a couple of spare tarps she could borrow. Up on the high road, the dips were full of water and the wheat fields on either side lay flattened by wind and hail. She'd been driving for less than fifteen minutes when she saw, at the edge of the copse off to her left, the blackened remains of a tree with a steady stream of smoke drifting off it. Given the amount of rain that had fallen, there was little risk of a prairie fire; nonetheless, she stopped and climbed up onto the bed of the truck and aimed her binoculars. She was surprised to see what appeared to be the ragged remnants of a tent close to the base of the tree. She turned the ignition off and went to investigate.

Some distance from the tree, a naked youth arose from the ground. He had his back to her. She watched him link his hands behind his head and stretch. She watched the shoulder blades shift beneath his skin, the long raised scars. She watched his buttocks harden and relax. She did not know what to do. She did not want to call out or frighten him. She just wanted to go on watching, unseen. The naked boy and the burning tree were an impossible conjunction in this familiar landscape, like something dreamed, with a dream's meaning. She could hardly breathe. The little copse had a spirit name but it had gone out of her head.

The boy stooped to pick up his clothes.

Please don't, she thought.

As if in response, he straightened and stood motionless.

Now he will turn. She held her breath.

And he did. His hair was a mass of wet twists; his eyes, wide with shock, were much paler than Grace might have expected. He was thin, his rib cage sharply defined. From just below his navel, which was prominent, a band of hair, fine as a dotted line of ink, descended to the sparse flat curls from which his genitals hung. His knees looked dusty.

Grace observed all this in less than two seconds, but two seconds was enough. The young man was a vision, with a vision's power—so unexpected in this landscape (*her* landscape) that she later wondered whether he had cast a spell upon her. The words came into her head unbidden:

coup de foudre, a bolt of lightning. How appropriate to this moment, as the tree burned and her soul burned too. All at once the boy exploded in motion, grabbing up an armful of clothes with which to cover his loins. He stared at her, frightened.

Grace found her voice. "I'm sorry," she said, holding out her hands toward him, as to a creature of the wild. "I mean you no harm."

The boy stepped back, shook his head, and said something she couldn't catch.

"I wasn't spying," Grace said. "I saw the fire and—"

"It wasn't me," he stuttered. "I didn't burn it. The lightning . . ."

"Yes. I can see. Are you all right? Are you hurt?"

He nodded, shook his head. "Is this your land? I'll leave now, only—"

"It's not my land. I don't own it."

"—my clothes. Are wet."

"Of course," Grace said. "After the rain."

He didn't move. They had reached an impasse.

"Look," Grace said at last. "What if I turn away while you get dressed? Then I can give you a ride somewhere. That's my truck over there."

She turned slowly, with a sense of tearing in her heart. *Please don't run off,* she prayed silently. "What are you doing here?" She needed to hear his voice.

"I was on the road."

"Yes?"

"And this storm come along. I took shelter in the trees."

"Where are you headed, if you don't mind my asking?"

"Vancouver."

Grace half turned. "Van*couver*?"

She felt him hesitate. "Is it far?"

"A fair step," she said with a small smile. "And uphill."

"Oh." The resignation in the single syllable was palpable.

"Are you hungry? Thirsty?"

"Some. Ma'am."

"I'm not ma'am. My name is Grace. And you're . . . ?"

"Beck."

"Are you decent, Beck? May I turn around?"

"I guess."

The exquisite boy had become a tramp, jamming his bare feet into wrecked boots while hoisting an old army rucksack onto his back. Sensing her disappointment, he apologized. "I had a hat," he said. "It got blown away."

She suppressed a smile. "Come with me, Beck. My place is close by. I'll fix you something to eat."

During the short ride Beck could think of nothing to say. He was sitting next to a woman who had seen him — studied him! — naked. The thought made him squirm.

She glanced at him. "I'm sorry I embarrassed you."

He turned his head away, to the cab's window.

The truck descended a hill and shuddered over a single-track wooden bridge. To the left, a valley opened onto rolling distances. To the right, light flickered through a line of trees. A sign fixed to two tall poles appeared and the truck slowed. The sign had two words on it. The larger, in fancy lettering, was *Ogygia,* although Beck couldn't imagine what it meant or how to say it. Below it, in plain letters: MCALLISTER.

"Here we are," Grace said, and swung the wheel. A track of tamped gravel curved between low hillocks. From the crest of one of them, a herd of horses lifted their heads to watch the truck pass.

The house, when it appeared, was a long, single-story structure of fieldstone and glass beneath a shingle roof. Close to it was a tipi, its skin banded with a red, black, and white design, its ridge poles splayed at the sky. From the far end of the house and at a right angle to it, a long tall fence wore a wet cloak of jasmine and honeysuckle; even before he climbed out of the Ford, Beck caught the heavy sweetness in the air. He followed Grace up the four steps to the veranda, one end of which was shaded by an awning. From within the dimness beneath, someone spoke. The voice was old and cracked but strong. The words were not English. Grace replied in the same language. Beck heard his name mentioned. The old voice spoke again, a short speech. At the end of it Grace gave a little laugh and turned to Beck.

"This is my *nah-ah.* My grandmother. Her given name means Walking Pony Woman, but most people call her Straight Speaking. Come and say hello."

The old woman was sitting in a cane chair with a walking stick resting against its arm. Beck awkwardly offered his hand. She did not take it and he snatched it back, blushing, before realizing that she was blind. Her eyes were almost shut, just two milky arcs below their lids. Her skin was as dark as his own, but grooved and crinkled like the bark of an ancient tree. Her white hair, thin on her scalp, hung in a thick braid over her shoulder. She wore a blue print dress under a shawl embroidered with a pattern similar to the one he had seen on the tipi.

Grace said, "She needs to meet you with her hands. It'd be easier if you knelt down. It's okay. She doesn't bite."

The old woman grunted humorously. "Not got the teeth for it anymore," she said in English.

So Beck knelt, and Straight Speaking leaned forward. Her fingers found the sides of his neck first, then traveled lightly down and over his shoulders to his upper arms, where her thin grip tightened. "Hmm," she murmured, lifting her hands to his face. Her fingers explored it like a paper spider. Beck fought the desire to brush them away. When she reached his hair she hesitated before carefully exploring it. Then she sank back and rearranged her shawl.

"You're a Negro."

"Yes'm."

"First time I saw a Negro was not long before my sight left me. Ten years ago. Soldiers, on a train heading east. They sang beautiful songs. My granddaughter tells me you're a fool."

"Huh?" Beck twitched a glance at Grace, who grimaced and rolled her eyes.

"Storm comes at you like a thousand horses and you

take it into your head to run to the trees. Which is the last damn thing you should do. Specially when those trees have bad luck hanging in their branches like the ones you ran to."

"I know that now. I ain't never been in a storm like that."

Straight Speaking cocked her head. "Where you from, Beck? That your name? Beck?"

"Yeah. Ontario mostly. Afore that, England. Place called Liverpool."

"Not Africa or the United States?"

"No."

"Hmm. The world is very mixed up these days. How old are you?"

"Nineteen or therebouts, ma'am."

"Thereabouts? You don't know when you were born?"

"Not exactly."

"Ha!" This seemed to please the old woman. "Nor I. I'm somewhere between eighty-nine and ninety-two. Can't say it makes a spit of difference. Anyone who might know is long dead, anyways. Grace, you still standing there? I thought you said the boy was hungry."

The food was some kind of cold meat pie with refried potatoes and greens. Beck couldn't remember the last time he'd eaten anything as good. The water was very cold and had a sharp yellow tang to it. The floor was of golden polished pine. A recess in the end wall harbored a big potbellied stove and a pile of split logs. Framed maps and photographs hung along the longer walls. From one of the windows,

Beck could see a distant glint of water behind a line of trees. Grace served the food, said something to her grandmother in the other language, and left the room. After a minute Beck heard the Ford start up.

Straight Speaking sat at the far end of the table, softly slurping tea from a mug. She said, "How's the food?"

"Good, ma'am. Real good."

"When Grace came home," Straight Speaking said, "she didn't know the difference between a mushroom and a deer's ass." She sighed. "I had to teach her how to cook when I couldn't hardly see a thing. It's a wonder I still have all my fingers."

When she heard Beck lay his fork down she said, "Want some more of that pie?"

"No. I guess that'll do me. Thank you."

"Hmm. You been traveling a long time?"

"A while."

"It shrinks your belly. I know that."

She heaved herself upright, using her stick. "If you're done, come and sit outside with me. That storm of yours cleaned the air. I'd like to breathe some more of it."

26

CLOSED MOUTH WALKING MAN

STRAIGHT SPEAKING SETTLED herself into the same chair as before and tapped her stick on another beside it. Beck sat and waited while she rummaged in the pocket of her dress and produced a small leather bag. It contained a short pipe, tobacco, and matches. With deft fingers, she filled the pipe and lit it. Her weathered cheeks hollowed into her gums when she sucked in smoke and swelled when she blew it out.

"You don't talk much," she said. "That's a shame. I enjoy conversation."

Beck said, "I guess I don't have a lot to say."

Straight Speaking grunted smoke. "You don't have a lot to say. Well, *I'd* say that an English Negro who's walked three parts the way across Canada and nearly got struck by lightning might have a tale or two to entertain a blind old woman."

Beck shifted uncomfortably in the chair. "I ain't used to talking," he said.

Straight Speaking lifted a hand. "I'm familiar with your problem. You don't know what kind of people you're talking to. That right?"

"I've heard stories," Beck said, cautiously.

"Ha! I bet you have."

She puffed an angry little cloud of sweet-smelling smoke. "Well, then. Me and Grace belong to what white folks call the Blackfoot people. Not that our feet are blacker'n anyone else's. We used to dye our moccasins black, is the reason." She waved her pipe at the horizon. "All this land, for days in all directions, was Blackfoot from when time was born. Except it didn't belong to us. We belonged to it. We lived the way it told us to. Then the whites came along and drew straight lines on their damn maps and said, 'This is Saskatchewan. This is Alberta. This is Montana. This is Canada. This is the United States of America. It all belongs to us now. You Injuns behave yourselves, you can have some little bits of it to live on.'"

She sucked on her pipe but it had gone out. Spittle crackled faintly in its stem.

"We tried to get along with them but they killed us anyway. They didn't need to murder us. That's what smallpox, cholera, and consumption were for. Starvation did the rest. The white hunters killed all the buffalo. There was nothing for us to overwinter on. A full two-thirds of my husband's clan died during the winter of eighty-three when the government didn't give us any food. Six hundred people."

She fell silent. Her eyes closed all the way down. Beck

wondered if she might have fallen asleep. It had been a long time since anyone had spent so many words on him. It hurt his head to hear them.

She spoke again. "I was born a day's ride southeast of here. My father was killed in a fight with the Cree when I was just a little girl. I went to live with my uncle's people. They were called Many Medicines because they were wise. My uncle's name was Old Sun. A chief. He taught me. When I started to speak out for my people the whites called me a witch. I liked that."

The word conjured up Beck's few memories of childhood stories. He looked sideways at the beak-nosed and withered old woman. *Witch.*

"I haven't seen my granddaughter with my eyes for a good while. She still beautiful?"

"I guess she is."

"Huh! You guess. She was kind of fat when she came home but she's worked that off, seems to me. Still got nice tits, though, wouldn't you say?"

Beck coughed and the old woman laughed. "You didn't notice. 'Course you didn't. You can lie to me out of manners, if it's a help."

"She came up on me by surprise."

Straight Speaking began to refill her pipe but changed her mind and let it rest in her lap with her thumb in its bowl. "Her mother, my daughter Alsoomse, went crazy and married a white man. He took her off to Winnipeg. You been to Winnipeg?"

"I come through it," Beck said.

"Uh-hmm. Grace says her father was a kind man in a troubled sort of way. I wouldn't know. I only met him once and it didn't turn out that well. He was a railroad man, and the railroad was another kind of trouble. Grace don't see it that way, but that's a different and longer story. Anyways, he died and left her all his money, so some good came out of the whole sorry business. Grace came back to us and bought this piece of land. She said there was nothing here when she bought it, but she was wrong. There's plenty here, but you can't see it just by looking."

She gestured with her pipe again. "This used to be a summer gathering place for our people, back when there was still hunting. Clans came from all over for the Okan. The sun dance. And to trade horses and arrange marriages and such. We kept on with the Okan even when the damn government made it illegal." She chuckled. "We still have a whoop-up here when the chokeberries get ripe. But it ain't a patch on the old days. You see my tipi over there?"

"Yes'm."

"I got that put up on the selfsame spot where I lay with my first husband on our first night. I wasn't much older'n you. I still feel him with me, now and again. Some things never lose their tickle. Ha!"

Straight Speaking fell silent. Beck thought she was thinking or remembering but she was waiting.

"Well?"

"Well what, ma'am?"

"Well, it ain't much of a conversation when there's only one person doing the talking. It's your turn. Tell me about your people."

"I dunno. I guess I don't have any."

"Hmm! So you sprung up full-grown out of the ground where Grace found you, that right? You never had a mother?"

"She died a long time ago."

"And your father?"

Beck was relieved to hear the sound of the Ford returning. "I never knew him."

"He died too?"

"I dunno."

The old woman turned her head in his direction. "Lord, it'd be easier to squeeze piss from a log than get information out of you. Who raised you after your ma died?"

"The Sisters of Mercy," Beck said.

"And who were they?"

"Not sisters and no mercy."

Straight Speaking laughed, a single harsh syllable. "A hard time for a child."

"You could say that."

The truck pulled up in front of them. Grace got out, leaving the engine running, and came to lean on the railing of the veranda. Beck couldn't help sneaking a look at her chest but the work shirt didn't reveal much.

Grace said, "Okay, Nah-ah? You been interrogating our guest?"

Straight Speaking harrumphed, then spoke rapidly in their other language. Grace answered. Her grandmother spoke again. Grace nodded. "That's what I thought, too. Okay, Beck, let's go."

He got to his feet reluctantly and picked up his rucksack. To Straight Speaking he said, "It was nice meeting you, ma'am."

"Oh, I ain't done with you yet. I'll still be here when you get back."

Confused, Beck looked at Grace, who said, "You won't be needing that bag. I'm not setting you back on the road just yet."

In the truck, Grace said, "Nah-ah said that if you were Siksika, you'd be called, ah, Closed Mouth Walking Man, something like that. I said you'd talk when you were ready, but she's got too old to be patient. Anyway, she can talk enough for two, wouldn't you say?" There was something bright and jittery in her voice. "I guess she told you our story. About how we ended up here in Ogygia."

Oh-jee-jee-ya. Beck tried to fix the sound of it in his head. "Yeah," he said. And then, "It was a tale with some trouble in it, seemed to me."

She glanced at him. "Not anymore," she said. They reached the road and turned onto it. "Nah-ah says that if you lose your own people you need to gather new ones around you; otherwise you turn ghost. You know what she meant by that?"

"I think so," Beck said. He thought of Irma and Bone. The thought stabbed him, as it always did. He hadn't seen them in more than two years.

The road turned south alongside the flank of a pine-topped ridge that gradually descended to more level terrain. The sun was halfway down the right-hand side of the sky. Peering ahead through the murky windshield, Beck saw, a mile or so ahead, a cluster of buildings. They looked like boxes someone had dumped in the middle of nowhere. Then, a couple of minutes later, two parallel gleams arcing through the low windswept billows of grassland. A railroad track.

"Cooper's Creek," Grace said. "It's not much yet. A coal and water stop on the line to Calgary. A depot for incoming and outgoing freight. A holding pen. The only farm store in a hundred miles either way. But we're getting there. Farmers are buying up land around here because of the railroad. An American oil company has been test drilling not far south of here. And over there, see?" She pointed to a group of cabins and tipis, smoke drifting from a couple of them. "Some of our people. Straight Speaking's people. They're here because of her, some of them. But they're smart. They can see the way things are going. The trick is to make sure they don't get swindled by the government every step of the way."

The Ford jolted over the wooden traverse across the railroad track and came to a stop alongside a long and low timber building with puddles in the bare soil in front of it and a gasoline pump. A painted sign running halfway across the frontage of the building read COOPER'S CREEK FARM & GENERAL.

Grace hauled the hand brake up. Beck reached for the door handle but let go of it when Grace didn't move.

"You got any money, Beck?" she asked.

"Some."

"How much?"

"Three dollars fifteen cents."

"Hmm."

He said nothing.

"I can't see you getting to Vancouver on three dollars fifteen cents."

The relationship between distance and money had unraveled for Beck long ago. You made it up as you went along.

Still not looking at him, Grace said, "How about you stay awhile and work for me? I need the help and we'd feed you, build you up a bit. I pay an honest wage. Enough to get you to Vancouver, maybe. What do you think?"

She said it in a rush. It seemed to Beck there was more to what she was saying, although he couldn't put a name to what it was.

He said, "What kind of work?"

She seemed unprepared for the question. "Farmwork. Animals. You any good with horses?"

"Not really." He thought back to the Giggs farm and shuddered.

"You can learn. I've got a good man to teach you. You know anything about arable land?"

He shrugged. "I worked on a farm awhile."

"Good," Grace said, and smiled. "You'll do. And Nah-ah says you have strong arms. So?" She waited like you wait in the pause between thunder and flash.

Beck nodded. "Okay," he said.

Grace let her breath out in a kind of sigh. "Good. Come on, then. You can't work for me looking like that."

27
CLEANLINESS ITSELF

THE INTERIOR OF the store was so densely packed with stock that, apart from a small space inside the door, the only room for movement was along narrow aisles between walls of crates, boxes, barrels, sacks, tools, shelves of canned goods, bolts of cloth, cupboards full of potions and ammunition, reels of cord and wire, piles of bed blankets and horse blankets, cases, cans, and cookware. There were four good-size windows in the long wall, but there was so much stuff heaped up in front of them that the light was dim; the air held a complex odor of wood, grain, tar, and a musty sweetness.

At the far end of one of the shorter aisles, a man was bent over a table, writing in a book.

"Hello, Ben," Grace greeted him with a smile.

The man stood and came toward her. He was tall and angular. His dark hair hung to his shoulders; on either side of his narrow face, a thin braid ended in a bead and a red feather. He wore spectacles.

"Grace. Good to see you."

"The tractor part I ordered come in yet?"

"Yep, and some mail. On the morning train. Train and the storm arrived the same time. That was some heck of a—" He saw Beck.

Grace said, "Ben, this is Beck."

"Uh-huh," Ben said, then spoke to Grace in Siksika.

She answered in English. "Beck's on his way to Vancouver and he's agreed to stop over a while to help out."

Ben nodded.

"But he needs clothes."

Ben looked Beck up and down. "I wouldn't argue with that. What's he need, apart from everything?"

When they drove out of Cooper's Creek, Beck had a big bundle on his lap tied up with string, and perched on top of the bundle a pair of buckskin and leather boots with leather laces.

Grace said, "Ben's kind of slow to warm to people. But he's maybe the world's best storekeeper. He knows everything in stock and where it is, down to the last tack and bean."

Beck was thinking about how she hadn't paid for the clothes. Ben had written it all down in a ruled book and then they'd just walked out with it. So Beck figured she owned the store, too.

They pulled up in front of the house. There was no sign of Straight Speaking.

179

"She'll have gone to her tipi to rest," Grace said. "She can't sleep anyplace with corners. Bad medicine gathers in corners."

They got out of the truck. Beck thought they'd go into the house but Grace said, "Come along. I'll show you where you're going to be."

She led him around to the back of the house to where a track, made just by people or maybe animals walking it, sloped downhill through trees and shrubs now coming into full leaf and flower. Butterflies waltzed through the air. In no time at all they came to a longish black-painted shack fronted by a narrow veranda with three doors and three windows covered in a fine wire mesh.

Grace said, "This is our summer sleepout. When we need extra help, this is where they stay. It comes in handy during the Okan, too." She turned around and looked at him. "The Okan is a kind of ceremony. It's—"

"Yeah," Beck said. "Your grandma told me about it. Something about a sun dance, goes back a long ways."

"Yes. Good. Well." She walked to the first of the doors and pushed it open. "I hope this will do. For now."

The room measured about eight feet by ten. Two bunks along the longer wall, with striped blue and white tick mattresses, a pillow but no sheets. Under the window, a chest of drawers. On top of the chest, a wash bowl, a jug, and an oil lamp. The light in the room was amber, and the air was hot and woody. Grace pushed the window open and plucked at her shirt front, flapping it to cool herself.

Beck set his package down on the lower bunk and hovered uncertainly. "Thank you, ma'am."

"Grace," she corrected him, stooping to undo the bundle. "Ben and his fancy knots." She dug into her pocket and brought out a clasp knife and cut the string with it. "Now then, what do we have here?"

She sorted through her purchases and selected a blue work shirt, a pair of American jeans with riveted pockets, a pair of cotton drawers with an elasticated waist, and woolen socks. She handed these things to Beck, who clutched them to his chest, fearful that this beautiful crazy woman might expect him to strip off and change into them in front of her. That maybe having seen him naked once she'd think nothing of doing it again.

Grace seemed to enjoy letting him think this for a moment or two, then she picked up the boots and walked to the door and said, "Come on."

When they reached the lake, shadow had stolen into its western end, but elsewhere the long swathe of water gave off sparkles that gathered and separated and gathered again. On its far side, multicolored reflections trembled as if in response to birdsong.

Beck stared. He'd seen a lot of landscape in his travels and wasn't in the habit of admiring it. Most of what he saw stretched miles ahead to the horizon, miles he had to walk through in various states of exhaustion, hunger, and fear to get to another long stretch that needed crossing. But this was different. He was staying here, for now, anyway. He could allow himself to notice its magic.

"Beautiful, isn't it?"

He nodded.

She led him to a shack, a smaller version of the sleepout, in the shade of a willow. Its front end was supported on two short pilings to counter the slope of the ground. Three steps led up to its door. It contained little: a low bench, a piece of soap, a mirror hung from a nail. Another door led to the privy. The only light came from a small high window.

"Okay," Grace said. "I'll leave you to it. Wawetseka will fetch some bedclothes down for you. I'll get started on supper. Go ahead and bathe. I reckon you've got half an hour before the flies come in." She paused in the doorway. "Come up to the house when you're ready. I'll probably not know you."

Beck undressed in the shack and walked down to the lake, wading in until he stood in the water up to his chest. He wriggled his toes into the soft silt between the stones. The soap smelled like cleanliness itself.

Special attention to your downstairs bits, fore and aft.

He shook the voice from his mind but obeyed it. *Nice tits,* the blind woman had said, and she might be right, as far as he could tell. He'd never seen a woman's chest. Not uncovered. He'd thought about Irma's, sometimes. He'd seen Bone stand behind her and reach around her and feel them. He felt himself start to swell. He soaped his hair and plunged his head into the cool.

Grace walked back up to the house. It was not good at all that he had awakened yearnings in her. And strange that he had been the one to do it. More than strange. Crazy. She was thirty-two years old, nearer thirty-three. He had stirred something maternal and protective in her, probably. The way she'd found him. Most likely it would pass. But she thought again of him standing naked in the swirled wheat, almost as black as the burning tree. He had come to her like some kind of omen, and she wondered what he might portend.

28
LIFE LESSONS

BECK ATE HIS evening meal with Grace and Straight Speaking, along with Grace's housekeeper, Wawetseka; horseman, Jim Calf Robe; Sonny, Jim's slow-witted son; farmworkers Tom and Jack (and Jack's pregnant wife, Otter Moon); and a near-silent older man whose name Beck couldn't pronounce but who didn't look up in any case.

The food was plentiful and well cooked: beef stew made with beans and good brown bread to sop up the juices. Beck ate like a man who hadn't had a decent meal in a year. He occasionally caught Grace watching him as he ate, and wondered at the mysterious agenda she seemed to have in her mind for him. When their eyes met, for the briefest instant, she looked away. But their meeting caused little ripples of pleasure that made him want to look again. What did his body know that he didn't?

At first his stomach groaned and clenched with the regular supply of good food, but eventually it began to trust provision of the next meal enough to divert nourishment to his brain. Beck had no way of knowing that starvation enfeebles the mind as well as the body. In this new life, he began to experience a mental and spiritual rebirth, began to blossom, like a desert plant after a storm. Even the jeans that originally slipped off his hips now settled comfortably with only a piece of baling twine.

Jim Calf Robe took charge of him, showing him how to muck out a loose box without having his head kicked in. Having mastered that, he learned to groom and clean and catch and lead a horse. He shadowed Jim, paying careful heed to the way he handled the horses, how he brought them in from pasture, how he approached them from the side so they always knew where he was, how he talked to them when he picked up their feet and smoothed their coats.

To his own surprise, the fear and revulsion he'd learned at the Giggs farm began to subside. For one thing, Grace's animals weren't flea-bitten and shit-streaked; and he discovered early on that if he didn't worry them, they didn't worry him back. Beck learned first to move among them quietly, without arousing emotion; before long he could lead six in each hand or have one move away just with a hand pressed against a sun-warmed flank.

From Jim, Beck learned that one horse needed to be approached like this and another like that. Slowly, over days and weeks and months, he found that each horse had a set of preferences as particular as any person. That some were calm and good-natured, others spooky and insecure, and occasionally one was so wound up with nerves, you always had to watch your back.

For a boy convinced that he loathed and feared anything with four legs, his ability impressed Jim Calf Robe.

"It's 'cause he ain't always talking," Jim told Grace, who wanted to know how Beck was getting on. "It's rare enough to find a kid who'll shut up two whole minutes in a row, but this one's got a passion for silence." He shrugged. "I never worked with a Negro before but I'd say he's okay. Don't need telling things twice. That's something."

And Grace had to admit that it was, and had seen Beck out with her herd holding nothing but a loop of rope, which he'd slip around some half-wild thing's neck and lead it in, quiet as Sunday.

Jim was happy, because ninety part-wild ponies need a whole lot of handling to be ridden and bred. They were tough as knapweed, smart and weatherproof as well as handsome, and men would drive a hundred miles to buy one.

"He's got a feel for the work?"

Jim shrugged, a bit unwilling to give his new assistant too much credit. "Seems to."

A relieved Grace nodded. It proved that she hadn't been too obvious a fool about Beck. Proved to herself, at least.

* * *

Beck settled into his work. He liked that if he kept still and kept his nerve, he could think his way into an animal, know the inside of its head before the animal itself had figured out what it wanted. Though most of what it wanted was food and sex, so that narrowed the possibilities.

When Jim Calf Robe told Grace that her best mare was ready for the stallion, she came down to watch the proceedings. Beck brought the mare in from the field and was walking her up and down, one hand on her neck for calm, humoring her out of her nerves. She was a beautiful creature, short-backed, high-crested, and intelligent with wide-spaced eyes and an interest in everything that happened around her.

"Get off your toes, Suki," he chided. "You got nothing to fear from that show-off."

And when the big self-important paint trumpeted desire at her, Beck chuckled and kept a soft hold. "That's just talk. Don't even pay him no notice."

But she threw her head up and whistled to the stallion anyway.

Grace wore a belted floral print dress and painted and beaded moccasin boots. Her hair was gathered at her nape and fastened by a bone comb. "How's my Suki?" she asked, and he stopped to let her see for herself. The mare was small, hardly bigger than a pony, with a thick black mane like her owner, a speckled Appaloosa rump, and soft brown eyes. She had shed her rough winter coat and gleamed with condition. Grace ran a hand down one cleanly muscled leg, then straightened and nodded.

"Good girl," she murmured.

It was near noon, hot and turning hotter. Beck's work shirt hung open and sweat melted in the V of his collarbones. Grains of golden dust spangled his bare forearms. Grace noticed with a start how tall he'd grown lately, and how poised. One winter on good food and regular work and he was no longer a boy.

"I hear working horses suits you, Beck."

He shrugged, his manner to her always deferent, a little detached. "No idea who'd be telling you that, Miss Grace." And he turned away with Suki and headed to the small paddock.

"Not Miss Grace, just Grace," she muttered for the hundredth time, knowing he couldn't hear her and even if he could, took no heed.

Beck turned Suki loose in the paddock while Jim walked Sago up and down by the fence. The mare pissed extravagantly, swishing her tail at him coquettishly when she was done.

"Nice, ain't she," Jim said to the stocky brown and white paint, who danced and called. "Let's just see how well you remember your business." He opened the gate and slipped off Sago's halter. For a minute the stallion stood in a state of high arousal, his crest arched, tail high, muscles tensed.

Then he stepped forward and lowered his head, snuffling the ground around Suki's hind legs.

"He'll be wanting to make sure she's ready," Grace said to no one in particular as Suki backed up into him, flaunting herself and lifting her tail to the side. Sago sniffed underneath her and pricked his ears, rearing up and snorting with excitement. The three of them watched as at last he mounted her with a huge heave and a glazed look in his eye, humping himself over her back, gripping with his forelegs and nipping at her neck. She lowered her head in acquiescence, accepting three or four strong thrusts. When he was through, he slipped off her back with his long flaccid member dangling loose between his legs.

Suki stood docile throughout the proceedings and, by the time he backed away, seemed to have forgotten all about him.

Beck blushed, aware in the aftermath how uncomfortable he felt being party to this scene with a woman present.

"No trouble there," said Jim. "And no reason she shouldn't take."

"What do we do with her now?" Beck asked.

"She goes back in with the mares," Grace said. "She won't need special treatment for a long while."

Beck turned away. He wished Grace wasn't here. That they weren't here together. Ducking under the fence, he pulled a rope through Suki's head collar and strode through the gate with her, out toward the field. Grace followed.

189

Despite her long legs, she had to skip a little to keep up.

"Slow down," she said, breathing hard.

Reluctantly he slowed. "I got lots to do," he said by way of explanation, not adding that he didn't have the luxury to idle away hours with the lady of the house, who often seemed to have nothing better to do than watch him work.

"When are you going to learn to ride?" She stood staring at him, her arms crossed over her chest, knowing perfectly well he'd do everything necessary for a horse on the ground, with no intention of ever getting up on one's back.

He half shrugged his answer, wishing she'd get back to her job and let him get back to his. Her presence out here worried him. There was always the strange feeling that she wanted something from him, and her wanting clouded up his head. Was his work not good enough? Did she not need him anymore? Well, if she wanted him to go, she'd have to tell him straight. Week upon week he was saving money, sufficient, if he lasted long enough, to get him to Vancouver when the time came.

Unless she had another motivation? The thought flapped noisily in his head and he shook it free. *A woman like that,* he thought, *needs nothing from the likes of me.* And he swore again to avoid her in case weakness should put him at a disadvantage.

After supper that night, as he was returning to his quarters, she asked for his help in the kitchen garden. They entered through a gate in the honeysuckle fence where she'd set large beds out to different crops: corn, potatoes, squash, beans. Half a dozen young apple trees were spaced down one end, adorned with clusters of hard green early fruit. Beyond them, a wire-netted chicken run and a roosting shed on iron wheels. The vegetable beds were fertile and undisciplined, overrun with weeds.

"It's supposed to be Otter Moon's job," Grace was saying. "But her legs have swelled up now that her time is near, and it's all going to ruin." She leaned down and hauled out a tall fat weed from the pumpkins. Then looked at him. "You said you know a little something about gardening?"

Paradise, eh, Chocolat?

He nodded.

"In Winnipeg, we had a French gardener who lived for his plants. I wish I'd paid him more attention. When we started out here I had to get it all from books."

They patrolled the beds slowly while she talked. It was a nuisance that the best soil was such a distance from the water. In dry spells they had to take the truck down to the stream, fill old oil drums, and haul them back up here. She said she was thinking of setting up a system of gasoline-powered pumps for irrigation. Or maybe drilling another well. The one that supplied the house wouldn't do the garden as well.

Beck was trying hard to pay attention but it was impossible not to think about the scene they'd witnessed earlier. Grace had watched the horses couple with arms folded and hardly an expression on her face. It had amazed him that a woman could stand and watch such a thing.

Do you have sin on your mind, Chocolat? Do your thoughts dwell upon wickedness at all?

She was squatting by a row of beans whose young leaves had been eaten to green lace.

"We need to spray with lye solution for the bugs. Weeding, planting out. I don't have the time. Just an hour or two a day." She stood up. "You reckon you can do that?"

"I guess." He disliked the idea of anything that put him more in her orbit, but he knew his evenings were free and so did she.

He thought they'd walk on, their business finished, but she took something from the pocket of her dress and held it out to him.

"Oh," she said, as if forgetting all along that she had it. "This is for you. Go on, take it. Straight Speaking beaded it for you."

It was a leather belt, coiled. Beck took it and opened it out. It had a brass buckle and elaborate patterns of beadwork that danced and wove along the length of it, intertwining in subtle shades of turquoise and green. It was a creation of great beauty.

"Pretty good work," Beck said, looking up at her. "For a blind woman."

Grace blushed, ignoring him. "That string you're wearing won't do forever."

Beck looked down at the beautiful belt draped over his palms. *It's only a belt,* he thought. But it didn't feel like only a belt. It felt like a lasso. Or a noose.

"You like it?"

"Yeah. It's real nice. I'll pay you for it."

She looked puzzled, and a little hurt. "It's not something you buy."

He felt guilty then, and put it on, threading it through the belt loops of his jeans. The beadwork made it stick and he fumbled the loops at the back.

"Here," Grace said, "let me." She moved behind him. "Hoist your shirt up a little."

He felt her tugging, the backs of her fingers brushing the bare skin at the base of his spine. The belt slid over his hip. She worked her way around to the other side, and then the top of her head was just below Beck's face. He could feel the perfumed warmth rising from it. The smell of her.

"I reckon I can manage the rest," he said.

She stepped a small pace away from him and brushed a stray lock of hair from her face. "It suits you," she said, smiling a little. She looked older when she smiled.

"I'll need manure," he said, shifting his gaze back to the garden. "Lots."

"The muck needs loading on the truck. Can you drive?"

"No."

"It's not difficult," she said. "I'll teach you."

He got the hang of it easily. Unlike horses, the truck was predictable. The first time he tried, they jolted erratically down the track with Grace bracing herself on the dashboard, trying not to laugh. Then they went along the tar road to the bridge and across to where he could turn around, and back home. Grace got him to drive down to Cooper's Creek and showed him how to pump gasoline into the tank and check the water and the oil. After the lesson, she nodded, pleased, and called him a natural.

From the veranda, Straight Speaking whooped, "A natural what?"

Beck stiffened and Grace laughed. "That old woman's worse than a big-eared bat for hearing things that aren't any of her business," she said. And when Beck almost smiled, she looked away quickly so he wouldn't see how pleased it made her.

29
INSOMNIA

A ROUND THE MIDDLE of each Saturday, Grace paid
Beck his money, along with Jim and Tom and Jack
and Wawetseka, and the old man whose name Beck still
couldn't pronounce. Grace wrote it out for him like this:
Ksiistsikomiipi'kssiiwa. "It means Thunder Bird in Siksika,"
she told him, but that didn't help him much. He could say
Thunder Bird but he couldn't say Ksiistsikomiipi'kssiiwa.

Beck kept his dollar bills under his mattress and the
coins in a jar behind one of the boards by his bed.

One afternoon Grace got him to take the truck down to
Cooper's to collect a shipment from the eastbound train.
The goods weren't aboard, but Beck took the opportunity
to ask about the fare to Vancouver. When the train pulled
away, he sat in the truck and divided the sums into weeks
in his head.

The truth was, he was starting to feel restless. He
thought about Irma and Bone sometimes, and even though

he thought about Grace McAllister more, thinking about her made him feel tied up in knots. He didn't know *how* to think about her. As a woman? Employer? Savior? Friend? None of it was right and it had started to make his head hurt even to sit across from her at meals. *Maybe she is beautiful,* he thought, *but she's also rich and educated and old.* And, in every instance, so far above anything having to do with him that even a pleasant dream now and again seemed wasted. Nothing he could dream, even in the privacy of his camp bed, ended except with him run out of town.

You got no business thinking stupid thoughts, a voice in his head said. And for once, he listened to reason. And yet he woke from dreams of her in the early dawn and put on his shirt and forced himself into his jeans and went down barefoot to the lake where a bird scuttered angry from a bush. He turned, anxious, but there was nobody there. Then he waded out into the freezing water until he wasn't hard anymore. He washed himself and waded back, returning to his room in the sleepout.

Grace was angry with herself because she felt foolish and she'd never felt foolish before, not even as a schoolgirl. Her father had taught her pride and she'd learned that lesson perfectly. Now, she accused herself of . . . what? What was the opposite of pride? Weakness? Self-indulgence? Or maybe something worse. A psychological disorder? A mental imbalance brought on by aging and years of celibacy and loneliness? At night she'd stand at the mirror and stare herself into submission, hands bunched in fists, telling herself to stop being such a goddamned fool.

She tried not to touch him or, at least, only to touch him when it seemed natural or accidental or appropriate. A hand on his shoulder or arm when he'd done well.

She was slightly ashamed of the belt. All the work she'd put into it. He hadn't known what to make of the gift. Nor had she.

She wasn't sleeping well. At dusk, Beck would leave the veranda when her grandmother went to her tipi. Lately Nah-ah had taken to needing his arm to help her there. Or did she? Was she taking him away because somehow she suspected? When they'd gone, Grace would quickly lock up and go to her bedroom. From there she could see the window of his cabin and would wait for the glow and hope for his shape to appear in it.

On hot nights she lay sleepless, repeating words to neutralize his hold on her. *Vagrant, hobo, orphan of the storm. Ignoramus, awkward, secretive, strange.* And, sometimes, *boy. Nigger.* After a while these incantatory and abusive terms reversed themselves into a language of desire that made her hurl the sheet from the bed.

One morning at first light she went to spy on him. She took a path that avoided the sleepout. It brought her to the lake thirty yards from the bath hut. She concealed herself and waited a long time but he didn't appear. The following morning, she was about to give up when he came down. He stood on the little beach with his hands in his pockets and stared across the water for a minute or more. He removed his clothes and walked into the water, shivering at first. Grace thought that surely he must feel her gaze on him as he washed. She held her breath. Something inside of her folded, collapsed: a feeling like hopelessness or release from it.

30
WILDER

A STRANGER ARRIVED. BECK was stringing young tomato plants onto supports. He was tired, having spent the morning with the yearlings and the afternoon in the garden. He hadn't seen Grace all day and a dull vacancy had taken possession of him. The heavily pregnant Otter Moon sat in the shade of an apple tree shelling peas. It was a peaceful scene and Beck would have liked to join her. A light wind blew from the south and it brought into the valley the mournful sound of the evening train.

Beck heard a car approach and park on the gravel in front of the house. He concentrated on the tomato plants. When he looked up, Grace was standing just inside the garden gate with a man wearing two parts of a city suit, the jacket slung over his shoulder hanging from his thumb. He was fair haired and handsome. He held a leather case. Grace said something, and the two retired to the house. Beck shuffled on his knees to the next tomato vine.

* * *

When Beck went up to the house for supper, Grace and Straight Speaking and the stranger were already sitting at the table, upon which documents were spread.

"Beck, this is Mr. Jerome Wilder, from Edmonton. He's helping us with a lands rights case."

Wilder smiled and raised his hand in a kind of salute. "Good to meet you, son. You the new hired man? Looks to me like you're doing a fine job."

Straight Speaking turned to them, her unseeing eyes uncannily clear. "He's doing a fine job all right. The question is, at what?"

"Garden's coming on," Beck said, ignoring her.

Grace glared at her grandmother. "He's good with the horses, Jerome."

Beck shrugged.

"Well, we're almost finished here," Grace said. "I'm serving up dinner in a minute."

Beck fidgeted. "You want me to come back?"

"No. Wait."

Wilder shuffled sheets of paper. "So," he said, a touch impatient, "we're agreed that . . ."

Beck watched the lawyer speak without listening to what he said. He watched Grace listening. Her left breast was close to Wilder's right arm. She was wearing a white blouse fastened at the base of her neck with a silver brooch. After a few minutes, Grace glanced across the table and felt a flicker of anxiety when she saw the direction Beck's gaze was fixed and the sullen look on his face.

She was right to feel disturbed. Beck's sense of exclusion was in the process of turning ugly. It had struck him like a nauseous spasm that Wilder would stay the night. A lawyer, an educated man. Rich and powerful. In the house. You could tell by the way they looked at each other what they'd got in mind. He felt sick with his own inadequacy. He wanted to run from the room, or stay and poison things. His outrage put stumbles into his breathing.

"Let's call it a day," Grace said, leaning back in her chair. "I guess we're pretty much there. Besides, it's late. We can finish this in the morning, Jerome."

Straight Speaking indicated Beck. "And old loudmouth over there mightn't be hungry but my ribs are sticking together."

Wilder clicked the cap on his fountain pen. "You're the boss, Grace."

"Thank you, Jerome. I reckon we've got a strong case."

"We won't count our chickens."

She smiled. "Would a drink persuade you to look on the bright side?"

"If you're offering, I'm accepting," Wilder said, with what Beck interpreted as a suggestive tone.

Grace went to the kitchen and came back with a bottle of whiskey and a glass and set them down in front of the lawyer. She went to the door and looked back to where Beck stood fuming.

"Would you please give me a hand, Beck." It was not a question.

He followed her. On the kitchen table there were two glasses with a shot in each. Grace went to the kettle on the stove. "I'm not much good with straight whiskey. I prefer it with a little hot water and honey, what my father used to call a toddy. How's that sound to you?"

"If you're offering, I'm accepting," Beck said with as close as he'd ever come to a sneer.

She turned to him, surprised, but he would not look at her.

"What am I doing here?"

"Peel those potatoes. Please." She stirred the drinks and handed one to him. "Try this first."

She touched her glass against his. "Cheers."

He regarded the diluted amber liquid in his glass.

"You have to look at me when we toast."

Reluctantly, he raised his eyes to hers. The hard resentment in his gaze pierced her. He switched away in a flash.

"Beck, what's the matter? Aren't you well?"

"I'm fine."

Grace sipped her drink. Beck took a gulp of his and shivered.

"That good?"

"Yeah," he said, then corrected himself immediately: "Yes. Thank you."

He stood at the sink to peel the potatoes. Usually he was good at keeping the peelings thin and not wasting the flesh, but his hands were unsteady and Wilder's plump assured voice from the other room tormented him. At the table Grace was chopping onions. The knots inside his body tightened.

Grace moved behind him and he froze. She pressed the side of her face against his back between his shoulders, thinking of the scars there, and the ones she couldn't see. He felt her hair on the nape of his neck, her cheekbone on his spine. His heart stopped.

When it began to beat again he heard her put the pan down on the table. The potato he'd been peeling had blood on it. He watched the blood well up on the ball of his thumb.

The next thing she said was, "We're nearly ready." Like nothing had happened and maybe he'd gone crazy and imagined the whole thing.

Wawetseka, Jim Calf Robe, Ksiistsikomiipi'kssiiwa, Sonny, Tom, Jack, and Otter Moon trailed in to supper. The conversation was general, about horses and crops and Otter Moon's baby, which was due any minute but which Straight Speaking said would be late. And a boy.

Wilder drank more whiskey and enjoyed the farm talk, joining in expansively and asking questions. Afterward, Grace fixed another round of drinks, the workers dispersed, and she, Straight Speaking, and Wilder went out and sat in the section of the veranda screened off from flies and mosquitoes.

Straight Speaking embarked on one of her tales, smoking her pipe. Wilder lit a cigar. Smoke formed lazy strata above their heads. Beck stood in the doorway and watched moths, attracted by the lamplight, dash themselves against the screens. These small acts of confused violence might have been taking place inside his head. The diluted whiskey had addled him slightly but had done nothing to ease the pain of his thoughts. He couldn't bear to stay, nor to leave.

Straight Speaking fell silent at last. Grace said something to her in Siksika. Beck assumed it was "Take Beck away, Nah-ah. We want to be alone."

But the old woman didn't reach for her stick. She only nodded and refilled her pipe. The conversation returned to the lawsuit against the government. Another language Beck didn't understand. Nor could he read the meaning in the occasional looks that Grace gave him. He thought about saying, "Well, I guess I'll leave you to it." He rehearsed saying it so it would make her feel bad while telling her he knew what was going on and didn't care. But he couldn't trust his voice to hold.

Eventually, Wilder seemed to become aware of Beck's exclusion from the talk, or more probably was discomfited by his sullen presence in the company. The lawyer sought to ease the situation by engaging the kid in small talk. He understood Beck had come from Ontario, that right? That was interesting because he himself came from there originally. Newcastle, on the lake. Know it at all? No, why would you? It never was much of a place. No, he'd never heard of Ashvale. Kitchener? Sure, he knew Kitchener. Until 1916 it used to be called Berlin. Did Beck know that? A chuckle. Guess they thought it politic to change the name to something more, ah, loyal, what with what was going on in Europe. And Windsor? You sure moved around, son. Yes, indeed, know Windsor well. What did Beck do in Windsor?

"This and that. Odd jobs."

Wilder leaned back. The kid's monosyllables were wearying.

Without warning, Beck continued. "I was a bootlegger for a while. Whiskey. We ran cases of it over to Detroit. Hiram Walker, good stuff. Drove it across the ice in the winter, used a boat other times. We sold it to Al Capone's mob till the Purple Gang took over and then—then, we had to stop."

Silence. Not even a moth hitting the screens.

Straight Speaking said, "Damn, the boy speaks more'n five words in a row. Never thought I'd live to see the day."

Grace stared. "Bootlegging? Beck?"

He'd shocked her and was glad of it.

"That was a rough trade to get mixed up in." Wilder laughed uneasily. "I hope you know you're talking to a lawyer."

Beck turned and met his gaze. "You gonna tell the police?"

Wilder laughed again. "You'll get nothing but admiration from me, young man."

Beck stood up. "Yeah, well, I guess I'll leave you to it.

Got an early start in the morning." The words almost failed in his mouth. He pushed the screen open and walked down the steps, wishing he could run instead.

Grace moved to follow him and then, glancing at Wilder, stopped.

At the door of the guest room, Grace said, "I hope you'll be comfortable, Jerome. You know where everything is."

"Yes. Thank you. It's good to be here again."

She said, "Forgive me, I forgot to ask after your family. How are Emily and the boys?"

"They're well. Charlie got the chicken pox back in March and looked a fright for a while, but he's fine now. Daniel's talking eighteen to the dozen already. I suspect he might turn out to be a lawyer like his pappy."

"He could do worse."

A smiling pause.

Wilder said, "It's none of my business, but that boy . . ."

She waited.

"I know you're of a, ah, a charitable disposition, but a boy like that . . ."

Grace looked at him sharply. "He's a man, Jerome. Does the work of a man."

"With a criminal past. I know a thing or two about bootlegging. It's a nasty business."

She smiled. "I'm not sure I believe a word of it, anyway."

Wilder was surprised. "You think he made it up?"

Feigning a yawn, Grace stepped back from the threshold. "I have no idea. But right now . . ."

"Yes," Wilder said. "It's late. Goodnight, Grace."

In her room, she lit the lamp, sat on her bed, and thought about the evening. Beck, a bootlegger? She knew so little of his past, except that he didn't speak of it. There were other mysteries. She'd caught him unawares, studying a book she'd left out, and felt a flush of pleasure at the realization that he could read. He'd shut it carefully, replacing her bookmark, and when she told him to borrow another if he liked, had thanked her with a neutral expression and left the room. A bootlegger. A literate bootlegger with more than his share of scars, visible and otherwise.

She had crossed a line with him tonight and it frightened her. The moment she understood that Beck was jealous had been like a silent thunderclap, a shift in the weather. His jealousy had been both ugly and absurd but it thrilled her. She could not tell him in words that he was wrong, that he had misread the situation with Jerome: that would have been tantamount to a declaration. He was an unbroken horse, half-wild, unpredictable because he himself didn't know what he might do next.

She thought of how he'd frozen at her touch, and knew that his outburst on the veranda was for her, not Jerome. *I am no one's boy,* he was telling her. It was the delayed thunder after the lightning.

She stood up, went to the dresser, washed her face and hands, and unpinned her hair, the little rituals that sharpened her solitude. As she undressed for bed, she caught sight of herself in the mirror. Not so old, she thought. Her breasts hadn't slumped; her belly was flat and firm, her waist and hips distinct and well shaped. She moved closer to the mirror and studied her face. Still good, but time and the implacable prairie climate had announced their intentions: in five years, perhaps less, youth would be a distant memory. Her hands were already older than the rest of her. There were things she could no longer wait for.

She gazed at herself, dispassionate. Was she really waiting? Or was this solitary life merely an excuse, a failure? Had she come to believe that being different required her to be alone? That independence meant she could never depend on another? And what about pleasure? What about companionship? Was it possible that solitude was the compromise?

She went to the window and looked out. There was no light from Beck's cabin. After a while she reached up and drew the curtains.

31
FRIENDLY LIGHTNING

H E WADED DEEPER into the water, breaking up reflected clouds pink-bellied in the dawn light. Bird music and the merest whispery shifting in the trees. Just ahead of him, a large insect jerkily skating the surface. He'd awoken with his mouth rank, his limbs dirty and hot. Last night's misery had barely been interrupted by sleep. He'd pulled on his jeans and come down to the lake thinking he might drown himself, and how it would punish her.

The water rose to his chest.

Last night he'd sat alone outside on the step and cried like an abandoned child. He shook his head, humiliated.

When he'd looked up to the house, there she was against the light of the window. In a rage, he'd jerked himself off, picturing them doing it, not knowing how to picture them doing it, trying not to think of horses carelessly mating, of Brother Robert. He cupped his hands and dashed water against his hot face, groaned.

Now it was clear to him why she'd pressed herself against him in the kitchen. It was a way of saying sorry for what she was going to do. She was in bed with him now. He took another step forward, slipping down the lake's steep shelf. It might not be hard to drown yourself if that's what you wanted to do, and he forced his feet backward. He couldn't swim.

The lake cooled his body but his head was still hot and troubled. He closed his eyes and took a deep breath, turning toward shore and submerging himself completely, pushing forward with his feet. With his head underwater he opened his eyes. Gray shadows shifting on the lake's bed. Diffuse beams of light. The water ahead of him murkier than he'd thought it would be, full of specks and motes of vegetable matter.

He breached the surface and she was there, just a few paces from the shore, naked, her arms out to the sides, the palms of her hands resting on the surface of the water as if using it to support herself. Her face was solemn. Beck stood paralyzed with shock, wondering if he had conjured her out of thin air.

But no. She waded slowly up to him, her fingers skimming the surface. "Beck," she said.

He choked. "I . . ."

And then she embraced him, pressed her body against his in the cold water so that all the warmth in the universe gathered between them.

She drew in a long slow breath and together they rocked gently, back and forth.

Gradually he untensed his jaw and leaned into her, listening to the way she breathed and feeling the blood pump through her body, waiting for his muscles to stop trembling, for her head to drop and his pulse to slow. The left side of her face pressed into his neck. He stared over her shoulder at a familiar scene turned inside out. As much to keep his balance as anything he held her, his hands firm against her flesh. It was a dream. His heart beat. Time slowed.

Last night he'd whacked off in a rage hating her, dear God.

She spoke, in his ear, "Last night—"

He interrupted. "Someone might see us."

"Come, then." She took his hand and led him ashore.

She retrieved the robe she'd worn down to the lake, wrapped them both in it, picked up his jeans and shirt, and ran with him, along a path in the woods to a clearing thick with tall grass. When they lay down together they were invisible.

She's planned this, he thought. *She knows this place.* But after that he stopped thinking.

God in his merciful wisdom. This unruly prong of flesh.

He closed his eyes and shuddered, his breathing fast and shallow. Then felt Grace's hands on either side of his face.

She kissed his eyelids. "You're beautiful."

He shook his head.

She leaned into him. Head on his shoulder. Kissing his neck. Breasts against his chest.

"I'm nothing."

She pulled back and gazed at him, frowning. "You're everything. Ever since that first moment. You burn in me like fire, Beck."

There was no need to confirm or deny how he felt for her. It was entirely obvious.

"I'm sorry," he said. "I can't help : . ."

"Don't be sorry." She smiled and kissed him.

Fits perfectly into the human hand.

He looked into her eyes. "I don't know what to do."

"I'll show you," she said. And she did.

It was all over very quickly. Grace was neither surprised nor disappointed. She had presumed, correctly, that he was inexperienced. There would be time, later, for her own pleasure. For now, it was enough, fully and joyously enough, to have possessed him. She felt that same sense of relief, of being right, she had felt when she first saw the valley all those years ago, and, another time, the inevitability of the naked boy and the burning tree.

Too soon after he'd bucked fiercely and cried out, he'd made as if to lift himself free of her but she wrapped herself around him to keep him close. After a while his harsh breathing steadied. The moment was approaching when they would have to speak. She rolled onto her side, taking him with her, then eased away so she could see his face. She smiled. "Was it good?"

It was a question that barely made sense to him. In less than a minute, an ecstasy of terror had erupted out of him and he had died and been born again. He felt tender and delicate toward himself and toward Grace. He did not understand her and could not imagine what she might do next. Perhaps she had what she wanted from him and now it was over. Or maybe this was a contract and they would be together forever. He had no idea.

He managed to nod.

She ran the palm of her hand down his arm. "What I feel for you cannot be measured," she said. "You are part of me. I won't fight against it. Never again." Her voice was so soft, he couldn't be sure he'd heard her words.

They clung together like people made new.

He stared at her and their eyes grew deep, pouring out a lifetime of longing. And suddenly he felt frightened, as if he were standing too close to a fire that would consume him, leave nothing but charred remains.

Sighing reluctantly, she released him, knelt, and reached past him for her robe. "I have to go," she said. And kissed him, and laid a hand for a moment on his chest.

Beck watched her disappear almost silently through the trees. He lay motionless for some time. Then the anxiety took hold of him and he scrabbled about for his clothes, thanking God in heaven that she hadn't left him to make his way back to the lake in broad daylight without them. He pulled on his jeans and boots. On the way to his cabin, the hissing and chirruping of insects seemed to make the warm air vibrate. As time passed and the calm logic of her presence deserted him, a panic began to rise in his chest.

* * *

Jerome Wilder, in shirtsleeves, was sitting at the table, writing. "Ah," he said. "I was wondering where you were. Early morning dip, eh? Great way to start the day."

"Yes. I'm sorry to keep you waiting. Have you been up long? Give me a minute to get dressed. Wawetseka will make coffee."

Her grandmother, thank all spirits, goddesses, and deities, had not yet emerged.

In her room, Grace stood for a long moment with her hands clenched in the pockets of her robe. The enormity of what she had done thrilled her. What had it cost her to approach him, to make her intentions clear? She would court disapproval; Lord knows what Nah-ah would say to her, she who could barely mention her own daughter's name after all these years. Would it be enough to make an announcement, to say to everyone (including Beck), "I have never felt this way before"? Of course it wouldn't be enough. Everyone knew who she was and what was expected from her in this valley. Everyone knew how she should behave: honorably, generously, sensibly. Sensibly above all. She was not expected to fall in love with a half-caste boy-man, uneducated and unversed in her people and her history.

Grace set her jaw. What sort of woman was she? And what did she have for a future?

32
STRAIGHT SPEAKING

GRACE APPLIED HER mind to the management of an affair. It could not be declared just yet, she felt certain of that. In Winnipeg she hadn't given a fig about disapproval, had almost invited it. Here it was different. She was growing a community to which she was central; she had to command respect. The people she gathered at this place trusted her, brought their problems to her. They watched her to see what they, themselves, could be.

It would be tolerated, she supposed, because she had the right to do what she liked. But it would call her judgment into question. When the men gathered at the store on Saturday afternoons they'd laugh about it. Ben would break open the beers and she could exactly imagine how the talk would go.

Well, Grace, she ain't been gettin' any for a long, long time.

Yeah, but come on. The hired kid? And her near old enough to be his mother?

The laughter might be tolerant, but it would be at her expense. At his.

All this she turned over, hour after hour, throughout the day, thinking about it one way and then another, wondering how they might be together, knowing that they must. She fretted the day away, retiring to her room so she could think of him in private, lying still, imagining his hands on her, the look in his strange green eyes, now clear, now clouded with desire, the intensity of his need, the passion, the doubt, the look, the feel, the him of him.

She needed him. But was it possible? Was it wise? They couldn't keep it hidden. People came early to the house. On evenings when there were meetings or gatherings, it wouldn't do if Beck was still there when everyone else left. And Jim might come to the sleepout on early start days and not find him there. Nah-ah would take him away and with her coyote ears hear him stealing back. Or leaving in the morning; she woke early.

It was intolerable to think of loving him illicitly. Who would respect her for that?

He wouldn't.

Around and around her thoughts spun. He would learn about sex just as he'd learned to handle horses; he would be just as serious and attentive. He might be slow to control himself. She sensed that he was not merely inexperienced, but afraid. Though she did not know why. He had lived many lives—that much was obvious. For a young man like him—no country, no family, no money–the world would have presented an infinity of cruelties. She could read that history in his eyes. But she would conquer him with a stubborn, ruthless gentleness. She would. He knew nothing about women or pleasure. Didn't he love her, too? Or did he give in to her because he could only do what she wished him to do? *Employed* him to do.

Her brain whirled. *Stop thinking.*

She'd reached no resolution except that she needed to see him, find where he was working that afternoon and take him away, touch him, kiss him, demand to know if he wanted her the way she wanted him. She had to wait. He might come to her if she stayed very still. But if she chased him, would he bolt? As she cooked lunch, the thought of seeing him again made her cheeks flush; her hands trembled as she set out plates. So strange did she feel that Wawetseka, quiet, discreet Wawetseka, couldn't help but watch from the corner of her eye.

"Are you feeling all right, Grace?" she asked.

Grace nodded the lie. She was not all right; she was churned up, dizzy ecstatic frightened insane. Not frightened, terrified. What if she loved him? What if he loved her? What if one but not the other? What if neither? Or both?

What would they do?

Her thoughts spun, taking her nowhere forward and nowhere back.

Nah-ah came in for lunch and sat with Grace for longer than usual, smoking her pipe, clucking over her own thoughts, saying nothing. At last she spoke.

"I need to see the boy."

"The boy?"

"The boy?" Straight Speaking mimicked Grace. "Don't sound so surprised. I got business with him. Alone. So if you could fetch him for me, I'd appreciate it greatly." This last was said with mock formality.

"Yes, Nah-ah."

Her grandmother ignored her as she went out.

Grace ran to find him, tracked him down in the high paddock. It didn't matter that he'd had sex with the owner; there was still a barn to muck out, dry hay to pitch up into the loft, leather to oil, the mares to feed, the youngsters to bring in, the fences to mend.

"Beck." She struggled to make her voice sound normal but Beck heard the anxiety in it as clear as if her tongue had stuttered and tripped. "Straight Speaking wants to talk to you. In her tipi."

"I'm working," he said, stating the obvious. He spoke without inflection, but looked her straight in the eye. "And I'll need to clean up."

"No need. She'll take you as you come."

"Will she? Why?"

Grace shook her head. "I have no idea."

Beck did not think this was true. Doubting her made him feel sick. He led down the mare he'd gone to fetch and Grace followed behind, jogging a bit to keep up. She could see that the mare was heavily pregnant; she'd be a mid-summer birth with a new foal coming into winter, always a risk. The mare walked, stiffly, with a pregnant creature's sway, her eye drooping, her back dipped. Beck talked to her as he went, telling her that the crazy old woman in the tipi needed a word with him in the middle of his workday and that's what you got working with old women. It came out as a burble of sound, more nonsense than sense and, as she watched him with the mare, Grace's heart caught in her throat. He ran his hands over the mare's flanks and legs; she felt his hands on her own flanks, her own legs, and shivered.

When he'd banked up the straw in the mare's box and checked that she was safe, Beck tied the rope across the doorway and left her without looking back. Grace's eyes were on him as he walked away and he knew it. He didn't show his own turmoil, his own questions. *What will happen now?* he asked himself, over and over, like a mantra. *What will happen now?*

Grace stayed in the barn, watching the mare, nearly still a youngster herself, could almost feel the straining, moving weight of her belly. She placed a hand without thinking on her own flat stomach, felt the powerful pull, strong as the moon's tide, on a place deep within her.

Recalled to herself, she thought, *Is that what this is? Is that why I've fallen in love?* At her age it was getting late. She grimaced. Nearly past it.

The interior of Nah-ah's tipi was a cone of warm amber pierced by a tilted column of sunlight from the open smoke flaps. The air was rich with the sweet autumnal smell of pipe smoke and bunches of herbs that hung, along with cloth and leather bags, from the support poles. Straight Speaking reclined on the fur coverlet of her bedroll, supported by a wooden backrest. Despite the warmth within, she was wrapped in a striped blanket from which her bare feet protruded like two narrow bundles of dried roots.

"Sit," she said.

He sat, and crossed his legs, and waited. The lower part of the tipi was a circular curtain of painted hides: birds, animals, a bear walking like a man, the floor space crowded with objects he could not identify. The fireplace at its center was a circle of stones around a small heap of pinecones and sticks.

"I had a dream about you," Straight Speaking said. "Which was a goddamn nuisance because I had more important things to dream about. But it's stayed with me, so maybe I'm wrong. Maybe you're important after all."

"Seems unlikely."

Nah-ah grunted. "That's what I thought."

They were silent for a moment. Beck fidgeted. He had work to do. "What sort of dream?"

"Be no point telling you. You'd never understand. Words ain't going to catch it, anyways. But you had many shapes. Some I knew; some I didn't. There was a part of it where you held an eagle's egg in your hands and it hatched and the eagle flew into the sun." She shook her head. "It's a powerful story. And it puzzled the hell out of me because you ain't one of us. You're not even what Old Sun would've considered a human being. On the other hand, you ain't white, so that's something. But on balance, who knows what you are?" Her hands busied themselves under the blanket and emerged holding her pipe, which she lit.

Beck waited. In the beam of sunlight her smoke unfurled and dissolved like milk in water.

"So this afternoon, 'stead of thinking about what I should've been thinking about, I've been thinking about you. About Grace finding you standing naked next to a tree struck by lightning like you were a piece of the storm itself left behind for her to find."

Jesus, Beck thought. He said, "She told you that?"

"Uh-huh. Other stuff too. About your life before you came here. Or got sent here. Seems to me you 'n' her do a deal of talking."

He shrugged. "Some. When we're gardening and such."

"And when you're screwing?"

He turned to ice.

Straight Speaking held up a hand. "Don't insult me by lying. I know what you're thinking, but no, Grace didn't tell me. She had no need to." Nah-ah sighed. "And I'm guessing you feel pretty pleased with yourself, huh?"

"No." He stared at her, angry. "It ain't like that." His wild heart was a stray dog, chasing its tail. He thought about Grace's face this morning at the lake and felt too churned up to speak.

Nah-ah sighed. "I ain't suggesting nothin'. If all this had happened yesterday, I'd have laughed out loud. But that damn dream came to me, and then there's the burned tree, and now . . ." She was silent for a time then put her pipe aside. "You still planning on going to Vancouver?"

That pang again. What was he planning to do? How could he even know what was possible in a life like his? "I don't know."

"You told me you had people there. People who might be waiting for you."

Bone and Irma. Waiting for him. He felt a pressure behind his eyes. A sudden, overwhelming sense of all he'd lost. "Might be." His voice fell to a whisper; his words sank with despair. "I've no way of knowing. It's been a long time."

"But?" She waited.

He looked up at her. Her face was unreadable. He suddenly understood why Grace had been strange with him just now. A wave of nausea nearly knocked him down. "You telling me I got to be on my way? That I got to leave?"

"I ain't telling you nothing. I got no right to tell you what to do. I don't run this place, or your life, or her life. I don't know if Grace knows what she's doing, but sure as hell she makes her own decisions. What I do know is that you can't be starting something like this and think it's gonna be simple. She ain't a simple woman; she ain't got simple needs. She ain't asking a simple question and as answers go, you're anything but."

Beck said nothing.

"So what now? You come out and tell the world? How they gonna react to that? You thought about that any? I ain't too happy about a future of the pair of you sneaking around, doing it on the sly. Ain't no dignity in that. 'Cause if a blind old woman can see what's going on, it won't take long for others to get wind of it."

"It ain't my place. . . ."

"No. It ain't. Ain't anyone's but hers. Hmm." The old woman felt for her pipe.

He said, "Are we done?"

"Yeah, *we're* done. For now, anyways. But you got some thinking to do. Thinking with your head, not what's in your pants."

He left her, finished with the horses, swept the barn, and walked down to the lake. Grace was nowhere to be seen. Misery flowered and ripened within him. He would have to move on. The astonishing welcome of her body was just another event, a mirage, a gift to be snatched away. Happiness, home—states of being that other people took for granted—they were as strange and elusive to him now as they always had been. The road was his fate; he'd leave here just as he'd left everywhere else. Dance to the west.

He felt like the blackened tree, lightning-struck, burning. Life would burn him until he was nothing but a pile of ash. Love would feed the flames.

He was late to dinner.

He was very late. Grace waited as long as was decent with a table full of hungry workers. At last they started without him. Her heart lost the desire to beat when it came time to serve the main course and there was still no sign of him. They finished eating and when he still had not arrived her soul turned to stone.

He *must* come.

She knew that he would not.

33
MOVING ON

THE ROAD UNFURLED before him the color of dull lead where it was paved, and dun where it was not. He could not leave her faintly, hoping she might catch up and beg him to stay, so he ran. With forty dollars in his pocket, in the direction of Vancouver with the wind against him and the trees hissing questions. He hitched a ride that took him north out of his way, which suited him in case she was of some mind to fetch him back, though in his heart he knew that she would not. Relief would be all she felt, relief to be rid of the problem she'd created. His mind refused to dwell on her.

Poor Beck. He had no experience to compare and no way of knowing that the look in her eye was not a usual look, and the way she touched him was not the way all women touched all men. He asked himself if the way she touched him was so different from the way Brother Robert wanted to touch him. During the hours after they came together, when he worked with Jim and pretended to himself that he might stay on, he more than once thought of her and found himself retching against the side of the barn when Brother Robert's rabbit face flashed up in place of hers. The only way he could stop it was to block it all, to banish her from his mind and know in any case that she had already done the same to him. He knew very little about life but he knew for certain that sex and misery went together.

But he knew Irma and Bone, who had taught him about love.

Beck shook his head. No love for him. He wondered with a touch of self-pity whether even his own mother had cared for him. He no longer remembered her face.

And so he walked and he rode, in the backs of trucks filled with animals, on top of trucks filled with hay bales. The world felt deficient of love, care, warmth, and light. Sometimes he had to shout merely to fill his lungs with air.

His body refused to forget her. *No,* he groaned silently, hating the awful living thing between his legs.

He pressed onward, toward Vancouver, listening for her voice in the wind.

Grace sat at the table long after everyone had gone. Nah-ah's ears swiveled and her brow furrowed with a dawning knowledge. Where was the boy? She tilted her head to the sky and could feel clouds gathering. Ah, she thought, feeling the direction of the wind. Trouble ahead for the woman who does not need any man.

She sucked on her pipe, thinking of her dream.

All her years of living had led her to understand more than a few things about men and women. Which left an infinity that still caused her puzzlement.

34

GATHERING

A MONTH PASSED. TWO.
Harvest was coming, and then the Okan.

Jim cursed the bastard boy who'd left him in the lurch when there was most need for good workers to cut and bale hay. Bad help was worse than none, so he handled the herd alone. Goddamned kid.

Straight Speaking would fast for all eight days of the Okan sun dance ceremony and pray for her tribe, the men and women and children of the dwindling Siksika people. She would petition the gods for health and fine harvest, for freedom and independence and dignity, and she would pray also for her granddaughter and the strange twisted manboy she loved, that he should come back to her at a time and in a state that would permit him to love her. Straight Speaking knew that her granddaughter was in the market for salvation, though Grace would have denied it with her last breath. Straight Speaking shook her head and cupped one hand around the bowl of her pipe to light it once more.

You would think it was Grace who was fasting, Nah-ah thought. When she'd taken the younger woman's arm last night, it seemed to her noticeably thinner than earlier in the summer, the elbow sharp beneath her hand.

"You planning on starving yourself so when he comes back you'll look like a dried-up old scarecrow?"

"When who comes back?"

Nah-ah snorted and shook her old head. "All the decent sensible men who've fallen in love with you — and not one of 'em good enough. That'll be on account of saving your heart for an ignorant penniless boy with five words and a shady past. Don't know who brought you up but it sure as hell wasn't me."

"Good night, Nah-ah," Grace said.

Her grandmother grunted.

Beck hitched rides, picked up casual work when he could. He asked anyone who might know, how much farther it was to Vancouver. Harvesttime made getting work easier: that was the good news, but hard labor for near nothing was the bad, and the thinner and wilder he became out on the road, from bad food and not enough of it, the less anyone wanted to give him work, and certainly not work with horses — not a nigger boy with those unsettling eyes and no people, no history.

He knew that as he traveled farther to the west, the work would disappear along with drivers who might give him a lift. The last man he'd worked for had laughed and shaken his head when he said he was headed for Vancouver.

In this way, time moved forward and he moved closer to his goal with infinite slowness, by inches and feet rather than miles.

Beck finished a week of farmwork and had been walking for three days on roads that no sane person traveled, not that anyone who traveled them — sane or not — was likely to stop for him. A thick layer of gray dust covered him head to toe and made his eyes burn with grit. He'd run out of food. The road seemed to snake out in front of him, featureless, more or less forever.

He hated Canada. He hated the road. He hated the memory of Grace. But most of all, he hated himself. He was nothing, nobody, alone in this godforsaken place. He'd found peace with Bone and Irma, and something like happiness for an instant with Grace, but nothing would last for him. He was a shadow, a sketch, thin as a blade of grass. Turn sideways and he disappeared.

He rode for two days with a man named Lester Floyd, who transported big rolls of asbestos for the building trade. Beck hesitated a second after the truck stopped for the driver to change his mind, but he didn't, so Beck pulled himself up into the cab, hauled the door shut, and slumped exhausted against it.

The wind drove rain with some force into the massive windshield of the truck, and the wipers failed to help much with what the driver could see. Lester mostly kept his eyes straight ahead, squinting into a darkness full of wet. He coughed a rough heavy cough at regular intervals but managed to talk through it.

"Where you from, kid?"

Beck thought before replying. "Nowhere in particular," he said at last.

Lester risked a quick sideways glance. "Everyone's from somewhere."

Beck shrugged.

"Have it your way," the driver said with a cheerful shake of his head. "I ain't from nowhere much worth bragging about myself." He chanced another glance at his passenger. "You'll excuse me for guessing by the look of you that you seen better days."

"Yeah," Beck said after a minute. "Some better. Lots worse."

Lester chuckled. "Well, that's what you get for being born a nigger in times like these. Next time, you be smart and get yourself born to a rich white lady."

The wipers swooshed. Back and forth, back and forth. Lester coughed so violently, it pained Beck to hear it. "You headed for Vancouver?"

"Yeah."

"You got friends there?"

"I think so."

"You think so?" Lester laughed again. "Well, I ain't going that way, but I can take you far as Medicine Hat."

"That nearby?"

Lester chuckled. "Give or take a thousand miles. Across the daddy of all mountains, not something I'd advise you or anyone else to try this time of year. Wet weather looks set to last a good while. Your best bet be to settle down somewhere till spring so's you don't freeze to death on the side of the road waiting for a ride that ain't coming."

Beck said nothing.

"You don't gotta listen to me, but I got more experience driving these roads than pretty much anyone you gonna meet."

When it became obvious that Beck was half-starved, Lester shared his food—canned meat eaten cold with brown bread. He poured homemade whiskey into two tin mugs, and passed one to Beck, sipping from the other constantly while driving, to control the cough. When it worked, the deep furrows on his face softened a little. It was cold in the cab; only the fug of their breath and the sting of moonshine offered any warmth at all.

The whiskey went straight to Beck's head and made him feel like laughing. Here he'd been smuggling top-quality Canadian Club across to the U.S. without ever tasting a drop, and now he was back in Canada drinking the worst sort of bathtub hooch and grateful for it. It burned like the devil going down, but it did somehow magic a feeling of warmth. He felt less gloomy with it looping around inside his head, until suddenly he'd had enough and dropped off to sleep, only waking when Lester pulled the rig over beside a tiny concrete roadhouse in the middle of nothing in every direction.

The place looked empty but spat out noise and drunks and gamblers all night long. Lester hauled a couple of rough blankets out of the space behind the seats and the two men lay down overlapping, feet to the middle of the big wide seat, heads by each door. Beck had slept lots of worse places.

He thought of Grace as he hovered between waking and sleep; he dreamed of her in the night; the first thing in his head when he woke was her. Later, he thought about Bone and Irma, brought up his memory-hoard of pictures of them, but something had gone wrong with it. Their faces were indistinct, blurred and bleached by rain. He wondered if they'd even remember him. If they were even alive.

The realization struck that he was doomed always to move on, starting new connections, ending them before they grew roots. He couldn't manage to see himself as a man with attachments and a life. Every stop he made was just a chapter in a longer, sadder tale. Did Grace really care for him? It didn't matter. They could never be together. That was clear enough.

He woke the next morning when Lester heaved himself up onto the step of the cab bringing with him good news and a great gust of cold air.

"Ran a few things down to Toronto in the back of my truck

for the grub slinger here," he explained. "He's got coffee with ham hash and eggs for breakfast. So rouse yourself."

Beck followed him into the roadhouse, which was blissfully warm and stank of beer. Lester's friend served up an enormous breakfast of hash, fried eggs, toast, fried potatoes, and coffee. A sign over the cash register read NO COLORED—NO WOMEN—NO DOGS but Lester's friend said that was only after dark, and anyway the boss wasn't around to care who came in for breakfast. Lester drank from his flask all the way through the meal. Inside the roadhouse, he coughed less and his chest heaved less when he breathed. His friend joined them at the end for coffee and a slug of Lester's home brew, talking about the crazy people coming and going and the poor son of a bitch found out back last week with his throat cut.

"Prob'ly owed someone money." He thought for a minute, then grinned. "Or more likely, someone owed him."

When eventually they returned to the rig, it was with bread still warm from the kitchen and smelling of yeast, so soft it didn't need soaking in booze to chew.

Lester started up the engine and poured them each a mug of hooch.

"That cure's gonna kill you if the cough don't," Beck said and Lester shrugged.

"Can't smoke no more; least I can do is drink. Ain't doing my stomach no good, you don't need to tell me that."

The sleet had turned to rain, enough to discourage Beck from leaving the cab except to wade out away from the rig and squat quickly by the side of the road. Even so short a journey left him soaked and shivering, and Lester threw the blanket over him with a shake of the head and a warning not to be catching noo-moan-ya.

"I been trying to fix this damn heater the last five hundred miles," he complained to Beck. "Sure would make life a whole lot more comfortable if I could." He coughed again and this time it took a while for his heaving chest to settle. The ancient rusted old gas heater looked to Beck like it had started life heating a horse and carriage and he wasn't surprised when, with a suck of air through his front teeth and a tut of disappointment, Lester failed once more to get it to light. "Damn piece of junk," he muttered.

They set off again, Lester sipping and coughing and talking as he drove, telling Beck about his granddad, a slave in the West Virginia sulfur springs, and his daddy, born a free man, who made his way to Canada to find farmwork. "And jus' look at me," Lester said. "I work for the company that owns this rig. Don't exactly make a deal of money, no wife, no family 'cause I'm always on the move. But at least I can say no one owns me nor ever will." He turned to Beck. "And you, kid?"

Something about the gloom and cold of the cab, the uncertainty of his future and the turmoil of his past made the pressure to talk urgent; Beck thought he may as well tell someone what had happened in his life, because he himself could make less and less sense of it. And so he told Lester about Liverpool, and the Christian Brothers, and the

Giggs farm, and then running away and working for Bone and Irma. And when he got to the story of the burning tree and Grace, he kept talking, as mile after mile spun away under the huge wheels of the rig. When finally he'd talked his whole story out, he stopped.

He didn't know how long he'd been talking, but it seemed like the largest expenditure of words his life had known and the longest time anyone had ever spent listening to him. The effort left him empty, physically weak almost, as if he'd done battle with a snake wrapped around his heart, and he slumped back, exhausted.

They drove in silence for some time.

"Why on God's green earth did you up and leave?" Lester's eyes were on the road.

The question took Beck by surprise. "I had to go," he said. "I couldn't wait around for her to fire me."

Lester guffawed. "Fire you?" he said, eyes wide. "Don't sound to me like that's what she had on 'er mind." He shook his head, chuckling. "Fire you, hoo boy. You got a strange idea about what women are like, don't you, kid?"

Beck wanted to cry out that he had no idea about women, no idea what they wanted from him or any man. Truth be told, he had not much idea about men, either.

"Seems clear enough to me what that lady wanted. And it takes an original sort of guy to turn tail and run, jus' when the big man upstairs's dealing you a royal flush."

Beck slumped. "She'd have told me to go," he said. "It was wrong."

"You think so?" Lester cackled and slapped one hand down on the big leather steering wheel. "Well, I know a thing or two about women," he said. "And it don't strike me you was in danger of being shown the door." He glanced at Beck. "I could be wrong, 'course. Been wrong once or twice before in my life." His laughter tailed off into a delighted hee-hee.

"She's older'n me, Lester," Beck said. "And rich. And leader of a clan. With responsibilities to a lot of people."

"Uh-huh."

"And beautiful." Beck muttered this.

"Well, now," Lester said thoughtfully. "What could a woman like that see in a kid like you? Not bad-looking yourself, I guess. Young. Good worker. Smart enough." He thought for a minute. "The reason any woman chooses any man is one of them mysteries nobody understands. But she chose you. And what'd you choose? To live on the road, head for a place a thousand miles away where you never been, in order to find a couple of people might not even be still alive and, if they are, might be a hundred other places than there." He shook his head once more. "You one crazy son of a bitch."

Beck's heart contracted.

"I ain't gonna be the one telling you what to do with your life, but I sure can tell you one thing. You look at me nice and careful. You look at my life. What've I got? One road in front of me and one behind and all the chances I had, lost. Not to mention a bad chest that's gonna kill me any day now, no money for a doctor and nothing a doctor could do for me even if I had. Your life don't get bigger on the road. It shrinks and shrinks till it's so small all you can see is that little square ahead of you and that bottle beside you on the seat. It turns you old and sick and lonely, and then the day you realize the road's the only thing on earth you love and it ain't never gonna love you back, it's too late 'cause you're just about finished." He coughed, a long ugly spasm.

When eventually Lester's breathing quieted, he sighed. "So you're planning on going to Vancouver to look for your friends." He shrugged. "They may still be alive. And then what? You gonna run booze with 'em in Vancouver till some lawman shoots you 'cause he don't like the look of your face or throws you in jail for nothing 'cept being colored, or maybe they gonna change the law so everyone can buy whatever booze they like and then you out of a job?" Lester shook his head. "Someone tells you they love you, you take it serious, boy, 'cause hundreds of women ain't gonna repeat that offer, even to a kid looks like you." He paused and corrected himself. "*Looked* like you. Your face ain't improved any being on the road."

Beck idly wrapped the fingers of his left hand around his right wrist and knew what Lester said was true. He was nothing but bones now, the flesh pulled tight across his face, skin covered with scabs and scars. He felt innocent as a child and old as the earth. He missed the lake and the sleepout. He missed the horses and learning something he could do. He missed the beauty of the place and the peace

238

of it; knowing there was food every night on the table. Kindness. He missed sleeping in a bed. Security. Conversation. He even missed the judgment in Nah-ah's gaze. No sighted person had ever looked at him quite so hard.

He missed Grace.

Most of all, he missed Grace.

Lester dropped him on the outskirts of Medicine Hat at midday. Beck refused the offer of another night in the cab, preferring to set off right then, hoping for another ride. He was impatient to get to Vancouver. And besides, he knew if he stopped any longer and thought about it, he'd turn back.

In the last hours of daylight, a few cars passed but none stopped. None even slowed. Night drew in and Beck walked off the road into a grove of trees offering minimal shelter from the wind and rain. He had a single blanket in his pack and half a loaf of bread, thanks to Lester. He missed Lester's moonshine, for the warmth it gave body and soul. He missed conversation.

It rained in the night, so hard that his clothes and blanket soaked up all they could hold and the rest sluiced off him. Beck tried to wring his blanket dry but couldn't bend his fingers to grip it. Not a single car passed and he wished with all his heart that he'd stuck with Lester. He might have found a place to stay till the rain stopped at least. Instead he huddled under the trees shivering violently until his body turned numb and his brain floated off to another place.

Toward dawn, he felt heat, crazy heat, and steam began to rise from his clothes. His teeth chattered and he soon found that his legs wouldn't do what he expected of them, so he lay by the side of the road shaking, waiting to die.

He lay still till the sun came over the horizon and then hauled himself to his feet, soaked with rain and sweat, half-crazed with fever, bones aching. His head swam with visions but he commanded himself to walk. If he didn't walk he would die, and he didn't want to die here where no one would find or bury him. One foot in front of the other, hour after hour, with the horizon changing not a whit so he may as well have been walking in place, talking to himself, laughing sometimes, counting out the steps to Vancouver with a little rhythm of self-loathing.

Worthless nigger.

Savage bastard.

Lazy. Stupid. Dull as day.

Wicked, sinner, orphan, fool.

Vagrant hobo vagrant hobo.

Fool of a boy.

Fool of a boy.

In as much as he could think straight, he thought Nah-ah was probably right. And Lester.

Fool of a boy.

Cars passed, but none stopped for the filthy, crazed-looking black boy dressed in rags.

* * *

Hours passed and at last someone stopped. At first he thought it was Lester, a similar rig, large and heavy and brown with tarpaulins flapping over its load. Beck had long stopped hoping for salvation; he had long stopped hoping; he had long stopped wondering why he was walking or where. He tried to move faster, to stumble in the direction of the cab, to say thanks and somehow miraculously to haul himself up next to the driver, to sit for a moment, to let the wheels carry him forward toward his forgotten destination. He remembered Grace, the word, the concept. Grace. *Grace.* He would have laid down his life just then for either.

He ran in slow motion, ever closer, never arriving, faster and faster. The cab stayed the same distance away. Tears of despair blinded him. *Move,* he told his legs. *Move.*

The explosion threw him backward off the road and with an ear-shattering *KABOOM* the rig burst into flame, a gigantic ball of fire roaring up from the cab in a wall of heat and noise. Beck staggered upright, hair and eyebrows ablaze. He watched in horror as a man climbed slowly down from the cab, engulfed; a fire, shaped like a man. The man-fire walked slowly to the middle of the road, and though Beck could hear nothing over the roar, he saw the burning man throw back his head and laugh. And so the man stood, arms outstretched, laughing, burning. Beck watched in mute horror for what seemed like forever, watched the fire embrace him tenderly, with enthusiasm, joy, even. And still the man burned, and laughed.

Creeping closer on his knees, he could see at last who it was, and it was the green eyes and the wild hair and the black skin that gave it away. He stood and watched. He stood and burned. Burned and laughed. Laughed and burned.

Eventually someone stopped, though congratulations were not due the driver, who would not have bothered had it been possible to proceed without driving over the body in the road. He opened the door, shouted at the kid to see if he was alive, and when an answer wasn't forthcoming, dragged him up onto his knees and, with difficulty, threw him onto the backseat with a sigh.

Life is just one damned Christian act after another, he thought bitterly. And then, with no idea how he might be affecting the flow of fate, he set off at speed in the direction the kid had come weeks earlier, the direction Beck had turned to face, just hours ago, at long last.

35
OKAN

THREE DAYS BEFORE the Okan, Grace woke with a heaviness in her limbs and a dull throb in her head. Most days began like this now, loss and longing and a deep sense of failure weighing down her dreams and waking hours. There was no need to confess her state of mind to Nah-ah when a blind man with half a brain could add up the disappearance of the stallion with the dwindling of the foolish old mare.

Grace washed and dressed and headed down to the road to welcome today's arrivals. It had rained all night, a soaking, icy rain that cleared the air and turned the dusty earth to mud. She scanned the fields, sore muscles testament to the work of bringing the hay in under cover last night before the weather changed. They'd managed it, but only just, working by moonlight as the wind picked up and the pregnant clouds threatened to burst. Most of the harvest had been saved, but her back and arms told the story of it this morning.

Damn it all, she thought, *I'm getting old. Too old to work half the night hauling bales.*

There was already a good deal of coming and going among the tipis, greetings and reunions, a group of men in shirtsleeves carrying clothing back from the lake. A car, a Model T with dim headlights, jolted over the grass and parked alongside the other vehicles. The light lifted. Above the eastern rim of the valley, the sky turned from peachy blush to azure.

Grace missed Beck and cursed him. She allowed her brain to dwell on him, closed her eyes and brought his face back to hers, his lips, his arms. His image floated in her head, and all at once there were flames, a raging explosion of fire and a figure alight. His eyes burned through the flames, boring into hers. Those eyes, green flecked with gold. *I will not be consumed,* the vision told her, and the hallucination was gone.

Grace stood perfectly still, afraid to breathe. She wasn't one for prophecies, unlike Nah-ah, who specialized in them. She didn't dare tell her grandmother what she'd seen.

Across the long yard, wrapped up warm against the morning chill in her own tipi, Straight Speaking tossed uneasily, dreaming of an unquenchable fire and a blackened tree that burned and burned without being consumed.

The few clouds in the sky were long and feathery, dissipating in a wind too high to feel. The people from the camp at Cooper's Creek came first. The lead wagon, long and four-wheeled with rubber tires, was pulled by two horses and driven by the old man named Joe Iron Pipe. Next to him sat his wife. The wagon was loaded with long white poles, bundles big and small. A variety of children ran and played alongside. One of the walkers had a shallow drum slung over his shoulder. Two more wagons arrived similarly loaded. Then Jim Calf Robe's truck, also with lodge poles laid out over the cab.

Grace brought food and drink and stood gossiping with the women while the men constructed tipis. Four lodge poles raised up, tethered at the top; other poles leaned against them, the painted hide coverings spread up and around them. All erected at an unhurried pace. Meanwhile, children formed bands and competed in running and climbing and singing and making a racket. By the middle of the morning, a dozen or so tipis and a couple of canvas ridge tents had reached various stages of completion. They formed a rough arc around an open area of grass. Grace moved among them, greeting and conferring, poised, chasing visions of fire from her head.

Straight Speaking was absent; as the Medicine Woman who would preside over the Okan, she remained in her tipi to begin the week of fasting and meditation.

The reluctant good Samaritan covered Beck with a coat and gave him tea and soup when eventually the fever broke and he awoke. His head was cool, and he was barely able to speak or walk or even to hold the cup offered him, much less ask questions about where they were and what happened to the burning rig, and where they were planning on going next. Day after day, the movement of the car rocked him back to sleep and he got what he needed most, which was rest and quiet and warmth. But every time he closed his eyes, he saw the figure of the burning man, and sometimes it was someone else but most often it was him.

When his savior no longer had to hold him upright to pee, he asked Beck where he was headed and when Beck told him, he raised an eyebrow and muttered, "Well, ain't you in luck."

Before dawn the next day, he left him by the side of the road, just two days' walk from the burned tree where Beck had first met Grace; and when at last he reached it, Beck stood and stared for a long time.

As he stared, a resolution formed in his head. *I will not be consumed*. Not with fear or passion or hate. Not with the past or the future. Not with an unwillingness to be loved or a murderous rage, or a sense of his own futility.

"I will not be consumed," he said aloud, before turning to walk, on legs that still felt like a newborn foal's, to the only place he thought of as home.

To his relief, the house was deserted when he arrived. His heart pounded with uncertainty and fear. *If she wants me to go, I will go.*

He went first to the horses. Jim Calf Robe was absent and most of the herd had been turned out to graze in the far meadow. Among them he could see Suki. Only a handful of ponies were left in, including Grace's own Koko, black as her name, and Nah-ah's old Aachuk, a big slow paint with white eyelashes. He wondered what they were doing inside on a day like this.

Beck left them and wandered out behind the barn through the dew-diamonded grass and climbed the low hill. The highest point for miles around, it offered a view out across the wide expanse of Grace's valley. To one side he could see the herd, wisps of steam coming off their flanks. Distracted from grazing by the scent and sound of unfamiliar horses tethered beyond the encampment, they harrumphed and stamped.

Below him were tipis, crowds, people arriving along the road. More were making their way across the valley. He felt his stomach lurch at the thought of a funeral. But the atmosphere was more carnival than mourning. A wedding? Jerome Wilder appeared to him like a barrel kick to the solar plexus. An urge to flee made his limbs shake. *I have no place here,* he thought, fighting the instinct to run. He dreaded seeing her and desired it beyond all else. He dreaded her news and required himself to face it.

Making his way to the house, which echoed with absence, he entered the larder and ate ravenously, like a criminal, like a man with a gaping void. *She must be below,* he thought, *greeting her guests.* Her wedding guests. She would have to tell him herself.

He went to the door, readying himself for their reunion,

but at the last second his courage failed and he allowed his legs to walk him along a bright corridor, his head full of the resounding silence. Cautiously, he opened the door to Grace's bedroom. The sense of her was overpowering, an opiate, her bed simple and square with a brass frame. He gripped the foot rail, closed his eyes and breathed, dizzy, hungry for detail. He tried to memorize the intricate pattern of the patchwork quilt sewn in overlapping triangles. He went to her dressing table and smelled the pots and bottles assembled on it. Her, her, her. Drugged and drenched and intoxicated with her, he opened her wardrobe and fought an irresistible urge to bury himself in the empty carcasses of her clothes. The intruder in the tall oak-frame mirror made him stop and stare. He was not accustomed to his own image, and the tall, gaunt stranger looked like no one he knew. He raised one arm to be certain, dizzy with vertigo. Who *was* this person? The reflection was hard and angular, too thin. No longer a boy.

A burst of drumming and calling came from a distance through the window. He hurried from the room, closed the door behind him silently, crept along the passage and out onto the veranda where the emerging daylight swiped him. Thank God she hadn't caught him in her bedroom.

If only she had.

What on earth would she make of the man in the oak frame? She wouldn't still claim she loved him. Not on her wedding day. Concealed in the shadows of the house, he surveyed the ground below—tipis, people, color, and noise; she would be there, with Wilder, surrounded by her people.

I will not be consumed.

He made his way down the hill like a sleepwalker, veering left toward the lake. He found two strange men sitting on the steps of the sleepout smoking cigarettes. They cut their eyes at each other when they saw him approach but said nothing. The older of the men looked as if he'd been left out to cure in all kinds of weather, a tall folded old bird, everything about him dark and sharp. He wore a Stetson over a bandana. The other was obviously his son, exactly like the old man but with more flesh on him.

Beck nodded at them and they nodded back, shunting apart to let him pass; they were anxious not to touch him.

His room no longer belonged to him. A leather sack occupied the spare bunk. Below the window, a knocked-about hamper or suitcase, wickerwork with a leather handle. From the curtain rod above the window dangled a threaded collection of feathers and bones including the bleached skulls of small birds. On the chest of drawers, a circular headdress of black and white eagle feathers set into a beaded band. Voices, Siksika, through the thin wall.

He walked down to the lake, taking the long way through the trees. Close to the water, a thing like a tent, like a slumped animal, had been created. Skins, hides, stretched over bent branches of willow. The dark gray ashes of a fire and a metal bucket near its entrance. Something rose to the surface of the lake and twitched back down, sending ripples in lazily expanding circles. He stripped off his ragged clothes where no one would see and submerged himself in the pure cold baptismal waters of the lake. The wedding guest would at least be clean.

36

UNFINISHED BUSINESS

BECK WASHED HIMSELF and his clothes, both so filthy they left an opaque ring in the clear water. Lake water, he thought, could cleanse a man's soul. He hung his wet things in the sun and while they dried lay hidden, remembering, in the tall grass.

When at last he dressed, he felt lighter. How undervalued was the pleasure of cleanliness. She would notice, of course. He submerged his belt in the lake, watching mud float out of a thousand tiny grooves to reveal the soft bright pattern of blue and green beads. It caught in his belt loops, a cool band around his hips.

Beyond, at the campground, he heard trucks and wagons approach the house. As people arrived, the encampment grew and with it the circle of tents. Cook fires were lit; smoke rose into the sky to the accompaniment of shouts and chanting, children calling, laughing, and arguing; the whickering of tethered horses.

He could not see Grace. He felt his otherness like a shard of ice in his chest.

Beck passed through the crowd like a ghost. They studied him, their faces expressionless. She was not here. He did not ask for her in case they would not answer him.

He went back up to the house, removed his boots on the veranda, and eased open the door. Dimness and silence. He peered down the hallway toward her room, skin prickling, returned to the kitchen, and raised the blinds. The stove was still slightly warm. He fed it kindling and two split logs and opened the damper wide, set the coffee pot on the hot plate. He sensed her presence before he heard her speak.

"How do I look?" The voice was calm, even.

He turned and his heart collapsed.

She was standing just outside the kitchen door with her arms slightly away from her sides, her open hands toward him, her hair in two long braids resting on the front of her shoulders. Long earrings, three tiers of narrow white seashells. The necklace, three loops of carved bone and turquoise. The soft deerskin dress was fringed at the sleeves, waist, and hem. Bands of elaborate beadwork, white, blue, and red, spanned her bosom. The pattern on her headband was similar, with a tiny beaded animal at the center of her forehead. She glowed in the half dark. Three long red blacktipped feathers rose from the back of her head like flames.

He didn't know her. She'd become some*one*, some*thing*, else. Behind him the wood in the stove's firebox caught with a *whoosh* that might have been his heart bursting into flame.

"Congratulations," he said.

She frowned.

"I hope you will both be happy."

She shook her head slightly. "You came back."

"Yes." He could not take his eyes off her. *I will not be consumed.* "For your wedding to that man."

"My wedding?" She took half a step toward him. "This is for Okan, the sun dance ceremony. Didn't you know?"

He shook his head, mute, flooded with relief and shame. His knees buckled and he crouched before her, head lowered, eyes swimming.

She gazed at him soberly, her eyes deep and dark. "I dreamed of burning," she said. "At first I was frightened. But it gave me hope. It was like finding you at the tree once more." He looked up at last and her eyes held his. "A sign."

The pain of speaking stripped him naked, made him formal. "You are the only home I have ever wanted."

She stepped closer and cupped his head in both her hands. He leaned into her hips and slowly stood, daring and not daring to embrace her. But her face shone and the brilliance of her eyes allowed him to forget what he feared, to forget everything but her. Once his arms enclosed her, he wanted to laugh, to shout, to dance. She pressed him close, her face against his neck, her breasts and body and arms and legs against his. Each felt how the other had suffered. Beck's eyes, impassive during his blackest hours, streamed tears.

"Thank you for coming back," she murmured. And then

she pulled herself away and took his hand, her face girlish, laughing. "Let's go down and eat with my people. Come."

They ate with Joe Iron Pipe's extended family, innumerable grandchildren and great-grandchildren sleepily milling about with bowls and spoons, gradually growing more voluble. Beck was the center of their attention; now and again a child would be brave enough to approach him, touch the skin of his arm, stare into his face, and run away giggling. Joe himself remained in his tipi; Beck could hear him speaking with his wife. He didn't emerge until the sun burned the valley rim and wiped the last stars away. When he did, rippled circles of silence greeted him.

Beck turned and gazed up at him with awe. Joe Iron Pipe's eagle feather bonnet added two feet to his height. His creased and hawkish face was framed by long lappets of white fur; ermine tassels adorned the sleeves of his richly dyed, embroidered, and beaded tunic; at his breast a sun circle made of bead and bone; in his hand a feathered staff with a buffalo horn handle. He looked like a god.

From the tipis, other men and women emerged similarly transformed. Ordinary undistinguished men and women became bird men, deer women; they were new and ancient; their colors glowed in the rising light.

A voice called from somewhere. A drum rattled out a burst of beats. Stools and mats and deck chairs were brought out and arranged around the periphery of the circle. People sat, changed places, settled themselves.

Grace led Beck to a short bench and they sat. He wanted very much to touch her.

A low murmur arose from the gathering. Grace looked away from him. "Here comes Nah-ah."

Straight Speaking stepped into the circle, lightly supported by two assistants. Beck would not have known her in the fur-trimmed and hooded elk-skin robe. Grace stood to greet her. Joe Iron Pipe did likewise, taking his position behind the three women with Grace. Straight Speaking pushed her hood back. The robe looked easily big enough to accommodate three of her; her narrow ancient head poked out of it like a tortoise. She spoke in Siksika, part speech, part song, reciting the clans. When she'd finished, one of her helpers spread a mat on the grass and she sat down. At the same moment, the sun lifted itself clear of the earth. The drummers kicked off.

For the rest of the morning, Beck watched. If he'd been expecting fireworks or a bacchanalian riot, the sun dance would have failed to impress. Two men danced it. One had on a bonnet of soft white feathers with two stiff feathers above his ears and two large jangly disks of shells and bones. He wore a loose red shirt. The other, younger, had a crown of leaves on his head and nothing on his upper body apart from a heavy necklace made of teeth. Both men wore skirts like striped blankets. It took Beck several minutes to recognize them as the men who'd been smoking on the cabin step a few hours earlier.

Two groups of drummers emerged from a little shelter

and began to play. At the center of the circle, six men, among them Jim Calf Robe and Sonny, sat around a big round drum and beat it with sticks that looked heavy enough to knock out a steer. Closer to the dancers' booth, four other men, all naked to the waist, beat a lighter and faster rhythm on shallow, handheld drums. The two dancers faced east and stared into the sun. The older man wore spectacles with smoked-glass lenses. Their dance consisted mainly of bobbing up and down on the spot, and while they danced they blew high-pitched birdcalls from whistles made of bone. At first all Beck could hear was noise, but as he listened, his breath and blood became part of the rhythm and he fell into a kind of daze in which he felt both lost and found.

At no signal that he discerned, the music stopped. The dancers retired to their bower. Straight Speaking was helped to her feet and returned with her assistants to the prayer tipi. The drummers relaxed, stretching their backs and flexing their fingers. Joe Iron Pipe approached the drummers and patted Sonny on the shoulder.

Beck surfaced. He was sitting among, but not with, the spectators at the periphery of the circle. Now a low hum of conversation arose. People regrouped, swapped seats. Children, many of them in traditional dress, performed little shuffling dances. He looked for Grace, saw her on the far side of the circle, working her way in his direction.

The dancers reappeared, the drummers resumed, and the whole strange mesmeric business began again. Grace sat down beside him and leaned close to make herself heard. "The dancers face east to welcome the rising sun. Then they dance to the west. Their whistles are made from the leg bones of an eagle and the sound represents the cry of an eagle. The old man's name is John Bull Child. He's seventy-two years old. The younger one is his grandson."

Beck nodded.

"Some of the ceremonial costumes are very old and valuable. The skill of making them is dying out. Joe's head-dress and tunic were made by his great-grandfather's wives back in the 1830s." She hesitated, looking over at her grandmother, who raised a hand in her direction. "Nah-ah wants to speak to me."

A little twist of fear in his gut.

"I'll come and find you after."

"Yes." He met her eyes, anxious.

He felt her hand grip his shoulder, brief but tight, and watched her walk around to her grandmother, watched her help the old woman up, watched the pair of them enter the prayer tipi. The door flap was pulled shut.

Nah-ah had not looked at him, spoken to him, in any manner acknowledged his return.

37
HOME

STRAIGHT SPEAKING AND Grace emerged from the prayer tipi. The crowd parted to admit them to the circle. Children were quieted. Jim and Sonny and their colleagues resumed their seats and took up their heavy drumsticks. Beck gazed across the circle, willing Grace to look at him, and when he found her eyes she smiled. Her face said, *I am happy. Be happy too.*

Though unwilling to look away, he was drawn to the figure of the old woman. When she pulled the hood back her face glistened, with heat, he thought, and exertion. Straight Speaking delivered a short speech, at the end of which her expression relaxed and she spread her arms wide and sat. Immediately, the circle filled with people, the melee quickly resolving itself into a long line, two by two, headed by Joe Iron Pipe and his wife. Behind the adults, children tussled for partners. The drummers hit a rhythm more stately than the fierce tempo of the sun dance and the line moved off in a bobbing shuffle. As far as Beck could see, the only non-participants were a handful of elderly people with babies or toddlers on their laps, a knot of shy-looking boys pretending that dancing was beneath their dignity. He tracked his gaze along the line of dancers, searching for Grace. There she was, laughing, resisting the attempts by a pair of young girls to pull her into the dance. She made her way over to him and sat down.

He looked at her, full of questions.

"This is the social dance," she said. "For couples. Some married, some thinking about it maybe. See the couple right in front of Otter Moon and Jack? That's Tom Day Rider and his wife. Her folks paired them up for the dance back in ninety-nine and they've been together ever since."

She broke off, looking past Beck to Florence Bear, one of Nah-ah's women.

He was far from able to read the faces of Blackfoot people, but it seemed to Beck that there was something grim behind the woman's smile. She planted herself in front of them on the bench and spoke to Grace in Siksika.

When she finished speaking, she held her hand out to Grace. Grace drew in a deep breath. She stood, took Florence's hand and turned to Beck, who supposed that Florence had been sent to take Grace away from him, that Nah-ah had passed judgment on their sitting together. He was ready to protest, but Florence Bear turned to him with an upward gesture of her free hand. Uncertain, he half stood and she took his hand in hers, pulling him up, leading them together to the line of dancers. A gap opened up and she pushed them firmly into it.

It seemed to Beck that there occurred a riffle, a tiny breakage, in the rhythm of the drumming; that for a moment time itself had come to a shocked halt. Then he was moving, without volition, like a leaf caught in a stream's slow swirl. His feet were clumsy; he watched them, trying to match Grace's. She gripped his hand tightly. "Never mind your feet," she said. "Look up."

He did.

"Grace?"

There was no need to frame the question. She laughed like someone gasping for air, someone surfacing from deep water. "We've been declared," she said.

They came alongside Straight Speaking, her face expressionless. She held Beck's gaze for what felt like forever. And then, barely perceptibly, she nodded. Nothing more was said, or indicated, or required.

They danced.

When the sun touched the lodgepole pines on the valley's western rim, three barbecues—steel barrels cut in half—were lit. Blue-gray smoke rose into the reddening sky.

Grace and Beck ate on foot, carrying their plates from group to group, family to family. Grace made introductions. Some of her people smiled at him; some did not. Some of the men shook his hand; others did not.

When the evening stars appeared, the musicians regathered at the center of the circle. Jim Calf Robe carried a guitar, Sonny a banjo, another man a fiddle. Halfway through their second tune, the moon ghosted into the sky and a chorus of bats flew across it.

Grace took Beck's hand. "Come on."

"Where are we going?"

"Home," she said.

NOTE FROM MEG ROSOFF

Did I offer to finish Mal's last book or did he ask me? I can't remember.

At the time, it seemed a simple thing to do—his death was unimaginable, so the promise would never be cashed in.

But he did die.

So I read the manuscript and went to work. It helped that I loved it, and loved hearing Mal's voice in every page.

I knew from the start that I couldn't write the way he did, but I could write alongside him, shape the narrative, develop characters he'd just sketched in. I knew exactly what to do, not because he'd told me (we never discussed it), but because the manuscript read like a guide to a landscape I intuitively understood.

It's a strange process, finishing someone else's book. If Mal had been alive, I'd have phoned him every ten minutes to ask if it was okay to change something here, edit something there, make a decision about plot or dialogue or character development. Instead, I was left to raise the baby as my own—with the invaluable help of Mal's wife and creative partner, Elspeth Graham. We made decisions that we hoped he'd have countenanced, perhaps enjoyed. The best thing about working on the book was how present he still felt in my life. Writing together was a conversation we could still have.

By the time the book was finished, I couldn't always remember which parts I'd written and which Mal had. The story and the characters and the most original and beautiful turns of phrase were obviously Mal's. Could anyone else write a line (muttered by the young Beck, upon discovering one of the Christian Brothers in the bath) like "*Jaysus, yer lookin' at a priest in the nip!*"?

Beck is Mal's book. Like all his work, it is bold and compassionate, unsparing, moving, and joyously, mordantly funny. Each page is shot through with Mal's sharp observations, his affection for human frailty, and his own gigantic passion for life.

I hope you like it.

I hope he likes it too.

AFTERWORD

Meg and Mal connected long before they met. They loved and admired each other's writing. As Meg once said, if you like a book, you'll generally like the person who wrote it. And like each other they did, or rather, love. Immediate friends, they had a lot in common. Extraordinary talent, love of a good book, and a good rant, great generosity and unending capacity for kindness.

They saw each other sometimes and talked on the phone often.

Mal was diagnosed with cancer in December 2014. He continued to work on *Beck* but soon realized he didn't have enough time to finish it. Meg said she'd do it. She'd finish *Beck* for Mal.

Meg arranged to come and stay with us in Devon, to see Mal, talk about *Beck,* and say good-bye. Mal died before she could make the journey.

That conversation with Mal about *Beck* never happened. But death is not the end of the conversation. Meg completed *Beck.*

I love this book. It is the extraordinary work of two great writers who loved and respected each other so very much. Thank you, Meg.

Elspeth Graham-Peet
March 1, 2016

SOURCES

Following are some of the sources that were helpful to the authors:

"Blackfoot History." Government of Alberta, Alberta Culture and Tourism. Last updated March 18, 2016.
http://history.alberta.ca/headsmashedin/history/blackfoothistory/blackfoothistory.aspx.

"Dancing." Blackfoot Crossing Historical Park, Siksika, Alberta.
http://www.blackfootcrossing.ca/dance.html.

"Indians of the Plains: Sun Dance Ceremony." American Indian Film Gallery. 1954.
http://aifg.arizona.edu/film/indians-plains-sun-dance-ceremony.

"Native Languages of the Americas: Blackfoot." Native Languages of the Americas. 1998–2016.
http://www.native-languages.org/blackfoot.htm.

Regional Learning Project, University of Montana–Missoula. "The Blackfeet." Trail Tribes website.
http://www.trailtribes.org/greatfalls/home.htm.

"Siksika Submitted Names." Behind the Name: The Etymology and History of First Names.
http://www.behindthename.com/submit/names/usage/siksika.

Steward, Julian H. *The Blackfoot*. Berkeley, CA: United States Department of the Interior, National Park Service, Field Division of Education, 1934.
http://www.nps.gov/parkhistory/online_books/berkeley/steward/index.htm.